WISHING SEASON

Books in the Dragonflight Series

LETTERS FROM ATLANTIS
by Robert Silverberg

THE DREAMING PLACE
by Charles de Lint

BLACK UNICORN
by Tanith Lee

THE SLEEP OF STONE
by Louise Cooper

CHILD OF AN ANCIENT CITY
by Tad Williams and Nina Kiriki Hoffman

DRAGON'S PLUNDER
by Brad Strickland

THE WIZARD'S APPRENTICE
by S. P. Somtow

WISHING SEASON
by Esther M. Friesner

WISHING SEASON

Esther M. Friesner

Illustrated by
Frank Kelly Freas

A Byron Preiss Book

Atheneum 1993 New York
Maxwell Macmillan Canada
Toronto

Maxwell Macmillan International
New York   Oxford   Singapore   Sydney

WISHING SEASON
Dragonflight Books

WISHING SEASON copyright © 1993 by Byron Preiss Visual Publications, Inc.

Text copyright © 1993 by Esther M. Friesner
Illustrations copyright © 1993 by Frank Kelly Freas
Cover painting by Frank Kelly Freas
Cover and interior book design by Dean Motter
Edited by John Betancourt

Special thanks to Jonathan Lanman, Leigh Grossman, and Howard Kaplan

Atheneum
Macmillan Publishing Company
866 Third Avenue, New York, NY 10022

Maxwell Macmillan Canada, Inc.
1200 Eglinton Avenue East
Suite 200
Don Mills, Ontario M3C 3N1

Macmillan Publishing Company is part of the Maxwell
Communication Group of Companies.

First Edition
Printed in the United States of America
10 9 8 7 6 5 4 3 2 1

ISBN 0–689–31574–0
Library of Congress catalog card number 93–71527

To all my cats, past and present: Benny, Cutesella I and II, and Paddington.

1

Horrible in power, terrifying in face and form, mightier than all the armies of the earth, the genie Ishmael streamed from the gem of King Solomon's ring and hung the sky behind his awful person with curtains of fire and lightning. Twin scimitars gleamed in his mighty fists, blue smoke poured from his wide nostrils, and when he opened his mouth the tremendous roar of his battle cry struck the eagle from the sky and chased the lion back into his den as if he were a pussycat.

On the plains before the high city of Jerusalem, the great army of Unbelievers saw and trembled. Their swords were as many as the hairs of a young man's head, their spears keener than a fishwife's tongue, their chariots swifter than the changing of a young girl's desires or the passing of an old man's days. They had come in their uncounted ranks to pull down the shining walls of King Solomon's city. Now they were having second thoughts about the entire enterprise.

In the rear of the enemy host their king turned to one of his generals and said, "A fiend incarnate! You never told me Solomon had a fiend incarnate on his side, Nahash."

The general stroked his artistically curled beard and replied, "Mmmmmno. I don't think that is a fiend incarnate, Your Glorious Majesty. Our spies would have told us if Solomon had any of those lurking around the palace. I think it's an ogre unleashed."

The king was not used to being contradicted. "I wasn't

born yesterday, General. I know a fiend incarnate when I see one."

"Ever-Living Lord of All You Possess or Covet, much as I dislike arguing with Your Supreme Omnipotence, I really must point out that fiends incarnate never carry weapons. I have an uncle who is an evil sorcerer with whom I used to spend the weekend, so I know about such things."

"Do you." The king's eyes narrowed and a nasty light glinted in their depths. "Well, any fool with or without uncles knows that ogres are eaters of human flesh. *I* say it's *not* an ogre. And I further say that *you* shall go forth to the very front rank of my invincible army to confront the creature. If it eats you, it is an ogre, and I shall admit that you were right all along. If it only tears you limb from limb you will *have* to acknowledge that it is a fiend incarnate, just as I said, and you owe me an apology."

General Nahash paled and began to shake. "Majesty, I— I think it may indeed be a fiend incarnate, as you have so wisely observed. There's really no need to delay our attack over silly little experiments which are quite unnecessary to—"

"It's a genie," said the general's personal slave. He was a bright young man, an Israelite captured during a minor skirmish while the invincible army was making its way to Jerusalem from the seacoast. Now he leaned at his ease on the general's second-best shield, shaded his eyes against the sun, and studied the monster a little longer before adding, "Yes, I'm not mistaken; a genie. My lord King Solomon is master of many such fabulous creatures. Everyone who is anyone knows that."

"A genie, you say?" The slave spoke with such easy confidence that the king had to believe him. "And—ah—do you also perhaps know anything about the—er—habits of genies? As compared to ogres unleashed and fiends incarnate, I mean."

"Well, genies never eat human flesh—"

"Oh, good."

"—or rend you limb from limb—"

"Much better."

"—when it's so much simpler for them to reach down

and pluck your head right off your neck before you can say boo, just like a girl picking oranges."

The king swallowed hard and placed both hands lovingly around his own neck. The general did the same. The slave continued to observe the genie, who was now stalking back and forth before the first rank of the invincible army, bloody foam frothing from his lips and huge sparks of green fire coming out of his ears. He had grown a second set of arms, the better to display a pair of matched javelins which had appeared out of thin air. When he twirled them, the sky filled with an eerie wailing sound, as if ten thousand widows were weeping for the soon-to-die.

The general's voice was suddenly very dry and brittle. It broke easily when at last he asked, "If—if that's how genies like to do their killing—plucking your head off, like you said—then why—why is *that* one making such a spectacle of himself with those swords and javelins?"

"Showing off," the slave replied, cool as northern snow. "All genies, you see, are the slaves of my lord King Solomon. Some he keeps imprisoned in boxes, some in lamps, some in mystic talismans. That one there looks like the jewelry kind: magical rings, bracelets, ear-hoops, whatever you fancy. If you spent centuries inside a diamond or ruby big as a pigeon's egg, you'd be inclined to do things a little gaudily yourself. Besides, the greater a show he makes of your inevitable deaths, the more likely he is to impress my lord King Solomon and the more likely my lord King Solomon is to free him in gratitude. It's been known to happen."

The king had not absorbed everything that the slave had said. "Deaths?" he repeated. "Our *inevitable* deaths?"

"Sure as taxes," said the slave. He jerked his thumb at the genie, who had begun to growl. "Hear that? You're making him angry. When he plucks your head off your shoulders, he'll do it *slowly.*"

"In all the gods' names, how am I making him angry?" the king cried out in anguish.

With yet another don't-you-know-*anything?* look, the slave explained: "It's the army that's doing it. And it's *your* army, Majesty. They're not retreating."

"Nor should they!" The general struck a proud pose.

"We have trained all who serve in Your Uncontested Magnificence's army to stand their ground, no matter what. Death is but for a moment, they are taught, but the wrath of their beloved and adored king can be made to last several months. They will not run, no matter how frightened they are."

"That's the problem," the slave said. "It would look *much* better for the genie if his appearance alone were enough to scare off the enemies of my lord King Solomon. Why, he'd be guaranteed his freedom if he did that! But if he has to put himself out to the point of actually *killing* all of you, one by one—well! It just isn't half as likely to impress his royal master."

One royal master was impressed. "Call them off!" the king shouted, his fingers digging into the eyes of the two carved gryphons that were the armrests of his portable throne. "Sound the trumpets! Give the word! Retreat, retreat, immediate retreat!"

The king's orders sent the general into a sputtering tizzy. "But—but—but, Your Peerless Splendor, what about the battle? What about the plundering of King Solomon's riches? What about the songs of praise that the court poets and musicians will write about us—I mean, you—when we return in triumph?"

A new growl from the genie's throat sounded like blackest thunder across the heavens. "Hear that?" asked the slave, studying his fingernails. "Now he's getting *madder.*"

"*To the utmost pit with the battle, the plunder* and *the praise-songs, you fool!*" the king screamed, seizing the general by his beard and yanking out half the curls. "I said we get out of here!"

And so they did, although in the confusion of retreat the general misplaced his third-best sword, his second-best shield, and one newly acquired Israelite slave. That lucky slave was only the first to begin the plunder of the abandoned enemy camp.

A great cheer went up from the walls of Jerusalem when the people saw the invincible army fleeing for their lives. The great gates opened and the people raced out to join the slave in tearing apart the deserted tents, looking for valuables. To reach the camp, they had to run between the legs of the genie, but not even the youngest among them showed any fear of passing so close to so great a monster. Like the newly freed slave, they knew that Ishmael was under the absolute control of their king and so was not to be feared while Solomon lived.

Finally, to the sound of trumpets, Solomon himself emerged from the city. He was carried on an ivory throne by eight princes. Four more carried upright silver poles that held a rich canopy of purple, crimson, and gold above the king's head. The throne, the poles, the canopy, and the princes were all liberally decorated with fabulous gems. As for the king, he wore no jewels except for a single ring whose giant ruby seemed dark and lifeless, as if the life had escaped from it.

Then Solomon raised his hands to his mouth and called: "Ishmael! Ishmael, my servant!"

The genie heard, and immediately began to shrink. Smaller and smaller he grew until he was only a little more than man-size. He no longer smoked or flamed, and his weapons had vanished along with that extra set of arms. He bowed before the king and said, "Behold, Your Majesty, how I have fulfilled your command." His voice was deep and rumbly, but nowhere near the bloodthirsty roar of earlier.

"You have, Ishmael." Solomon smiled. "And fulfilled it admirably. You have my thanks. Now, to celebrate this victory, I wish for you to bring here a royal banquet. Let there be tables of gold and silver covered with silk. Let there be meat and drink of every kind. Let there be enough so that every citizen of Jerusalem may come and be satisfied and come again when next he is hungry and—"

"No," said the genie.

King Solomon frowned. " 'No'?" He repeated the word as if pretending he'd misheard it would change it.

Ishmael spread his powerfully muscled hands. "If Your Majesty will recall, when you first acquired me you wished for me to help with the construction of the Temple. Then you wished for me to fetch a suitable gift for the Queen of

Sheba as a souvenir of her visit to Jerusalem. Last of all, there was today's wish. That's three. And that's all."

King Solomon began to turn the color of his canopy, but Ishmael remained firm. "I told you the rules when you first called me out of the ring: Three wishes, and *no* using one of those three to wish for more wishes. You agreed, you wished, I complied, and now I am free."

King Solomon drummed his fingers on the arm of his ivory throne. "Even knowing that I possess powers to command the Armies of the Air to destroy you where you stand, you refuse me?"

The genie folded his arms. "You knew the terms. Fair is fair. And since you *do* have more than your share of magical beings to serve you, I think it would be selfish of you to fight over so small a thing as my freedom."

King Solomon considered this. "Fair is fair," he agreed. "And truth is truth. Behold! You value your freedom more than your existence, yet you value what is *fair* more than your freedom. Is it so?"

"Precisely, O Wisest of Earthly Monarchs." Ishmael bowed more elaborately this time.

"Oh," said King Solomon. He pulled the ruby ring from his finger. "You'll be wanting this back, I suppose."

"If it is not too great an inconvenience, Majesty."

"No, no, not at all." He flipped the ring high into the air and remarked, "Catch."

The ring spun in the sunlight, a blur of blood-red and gold. As it tumbled against the bright blue sky, it slowed in its flight, climbing and climbing, never reaching the top of its arc, never beginning the fall back to earth. Its outline became fuzzy. Small glints of ruby-colored light broke away from the great jewel, filling the sky with free-falling flakes of brilliance. The lights multiplied until all that could be seen was a blizzard of scarlet brightness. King Solomon disappeared behind the sparkling veil, the towers of Jerusalem vanished, and the whole world was swallowed in a scarlet haze.

"Teacher! Teacher! I can't see what King Solomon is doing!"

Ishmael turned from the fading vision of past glory that

he had conjured up for his students and sighed. Really, this new generation of genies was quite without any appreciation for a really *artistic* ending.

With infinite patience he answered, "There is nothing more to see, Gamal. The vision has made my point. And what do you think that point is?" He raised his bushy gray eyebrows and regarded his unpromising pupil hopefully.

Gamal shifted uncomfortably on his flying carpet, making it buck and dip in mid-air. Although genies could change their looks, they could not change them *entirely*. An ugly genie could transform himself into a horse, but it would be an ugly horse. Gamal would make a *very* ugly horse. He was big and beefy, with a flat, sallow face that always seemed to be frozen in a sulky frown. He mumbled something which was not the correct answer.

There was a ripple of laughter from the other young genies in the classroom. It stopped abruptly when Gamal glared at them. He had a reputation as a cheater of mortals, a liar, and a brat, but mostly as a bully.

Only one of the assembled genies did not stop laughing at Gamal. This was because he had never started. He lay comfortably on a lush blue-and-green carpet that hovered in the corner of the classroom nearest to the garden window. Clearly he held himself to be above these petty schoolday squabbles. A little leather-bound book of poetry was in his hand. Without bothering to look up from it he said:

"Your point, O Teacher, is that no matter how high and mighty the mortal master we serve, our first duty is loyalty to the rules that limit our magic. Even if it means putting ourselves in danger." He raised his handsome face from the book and his honey-colored eyes twinkled with a smile. "After all, fair is fair."

"Well said, Khalid!" Ishmael could not hide the pride he felt for this, his best student. The lad was—what?—no more than a century and a half old, yet he had easily mastered every lesson of Advanced Hearkening and Obedience, lessons it took other genies half a millennium to complete.

If only he did not know *how smart he is,* Ishmael thought. *Ah, well! I suppose he has good reason to be so vain.* A teasing voice whispered in the elder genie's ear, *Pride*

goeth before destruction, and a haughty spirit before a fall.
"Oh, shut up, Majesty," he muttered to King Solomon's
ghost.

A hand shot up in the back of the classroom and a sweet,
musical voice said, "O Revered Teacher, the vision likewise
shows us that no matter how high and mighty the mortal
master we find, we must always be certain to state that he
or she is entitled to three wishes, three wishes only, and
none of these may be used to wish for more wishes."

Khalid sniffed. "I didn't think I needed to mention something so obvious, so . . . *elementary.*" He went back to his
poems.

Ishmael clapped his hands together and, to punish his
uncalled-for sneering, Khalid's book vanished in a blaze of
blue fire. After the necessary reprimanding frown at a startled Khalid, the teacher's smiles were all for the pretty genie
maiden, Tamar. The lass was often Khalid's equal in the
classroom, yet modest where he was smug. "You are right,
Tamar," Ishmael said. "What is vital is often elementary. It
was careless to have forgotten mentioning the *However*
clause." He looked at Khalid meaningfully.

"I did not forget it," Khalid maintained. "I simply didn't
think—"

"*That's* for sure." Gamal snickered nastily.

"At least Khalid didn't say that the point of our teacher's
lesson was how to pluck the heads off mortals," Tamar
snapped. Her flying carpet rose with her temper until her
dark curls nearly brushed the domed ceiling.

So much fire, Ishmael mused as he observed Tamar's
heated defense of Khalid. *Beauty and brains to match.* He
clicked his tongue. *I wonder how many centuries will pass
before she realizes that Khalid notices none of it?*

It was all very depressing, and Ishmael had one time-
proven cure for sorrow. "For tomorrow, practice making blue
smoke come out of your nostrils, bloody foam from your
mouths, and green fire from your ears. Class dismissed!"

The young genies leaped from their carpets and bowed
the moment that their feet touched the tiled floor. "HEAR-
KENING AND OBEDIENCE," they all cried as one, and van-

ished. This time only five of them neglected to make their hats disappear too.

Ishmael chuckled over the forgetfulness of youth as he gathered up the castoff turbans and veils. A snap of his fingers sent them flying back to their owners. Then he went out into the garden to sit beside the fountain pool, feed tidbits to the goldfish, and forget the quirks and failings of his students.

"They will learn better once they have cut their teeth on the real world," he told the fat fish. They rolled their goggly black eyes at him, opening and shutting their mouths, saying nothing. "I only hope it comes in time for Khalid. If his head gets any bigger, soon he won't be able to get it through the classroom door. He's certainly bright enough to enter the wishing business—an even chance whether he or Tamar will be the first to graduate, in fact. Once out there, he'll find out that book-learning doesn't give you all the answers for dealing with humans. Yes, after the first encounter with a mortal, everything falls right into perspective."

Ishmael grew suddenly thoughtful. A notion had lodged itself in his mind, and the longer it stayed, the more attractive it became. "Yes," he said to himself. "Yes, of course, that might be just what he needs. Khalid!"

"You summoned me, O Teacher?" Khalid was seated beside the older genie almost before Ishmael had finished shouting his name into the air. He looked as cool as if he had been there all along.

Ishmael beamed and patted his best student on the shoulder. "Khalid, my lad, I have good news for you. . . ."

2

"—Into a *lamp*? Oh, Khalid, that's wonderful!" Tamar clapped her hands together and gazed at him with undisguised admiration. As Ishmael had already observed, Khalid remained entirely unaware of the genie maiden's affection.

"Yes, isn't it?" he replied, basking in the congratulations of his fellow students. Ishmael's pupils had gathered at their usual after-school spot to sip sweet sherbet drinks and watch the unicorn races. Ever since Khalid's announcement, however, no one paid any attention to the race. "He said it's the custom to assign new genies to rings, but because I show such promise, he's lending me his very own lamp for a trial run. If I succeed in correctly granting wishes to one human being, I go straight into a lamp of my own."

"Straight into a stewpot's where *you* belong," Gamal grumbled. The big genie's face darkened with hate as he saw how Tamar still hung onto that obnoxious Khalid's every word. *Brains aren't everything,* he thought bitterly. *In a fair battle of magics I could take that pretty little rosebud Khalid and snap his stem in two. And in a battle of magics the way I like them, there'd be nothing left of him but a few worm-eaten petals and a gooey black smudge.*

Tamar sighed. "I wonder how long it'll be before I earn my own lamp? I've heard those rings can be so crowded, hardly any storage space, and no room at all to raise a family . . ." She let her voice drift off suggestively, her eyes on Khalid.

"Oh, I'm sure Master Ishmael thinks you're bright enough to be assigned to a brass bottle, not a ring," Khalid said, missing any and all hints Tamar might send his way. "Well, I must be off. The lamp awaits." He made the briefest of bows to his classmates and began to dematerialize.

"I hope your first master's kind!" Tamar called after him.

"Why shouldn't he be?" Khalid responded. "All mortals are pretty much alike."

"What? All mortals *alike*?" Tamar's eyes were wide. "Not by a long shot! Weren't you in class when we studied—? That's right, you weren't. Khalid, wait, you really ought to know! Why, there's males and females, tall and short, clean-faced and whiskered, bald and hairy, hair curled or straight, hair, eyes, *and* skin in so very many colors you can't begin to count them, some whose eyes cannot see, some whose ears are incapable of hearing, some who run, some who cannot even crawl—"

"Yes, yes, I *know* all that." Khalid's body was mist from the waist down. The vanishing effect climbed swiftly up until his last words before it reached his mouth were, "You'd think I wouldn't know a mortal when I saw one!"

Khalid lay scrunched up within Ishmael's lamp and wondered how his teacher had managed to squeeze into a ring. It was not only cramped in the lamp, it was boring. The worst part was not knowing how long his captivity might last. Senior genies did not have to inhabit their lamps at all times. Only junior-grade genies had to stay within the objects containing them, until they had proved themselves to their elders. They could not afford to take the chance of being so far away that they missed a summons. Experienced genies like Ishmael had senses so trained that they might fly to their proper places the moment some lucky mortal found the lamp and rubbed it. Until then, they were free to enjoy the gardens, orchards, palaces, and ten thousand other pleasures of the genie homeland.

The result of this arrangement was that no senior genie knew where in the mortal world his lamp was. For all Ishmael could tell, this lamp he'd sent Khalid to inhabit was at the bottom of the sea, or buried in the ruins of an earthquake. On the other hand, it might be sitting in some merchant's shop, or already in the possession of the mortal destined to rub it and get the surprise of his life.

"May it be so," Khalid muttered to himself. He squirmed against the cold metal walls. "Master Ishmael is a great teacher, but I don't care for his taste in furnishing a lamp. When I get one of my own, I shall ask for something a little more cushiony and comfortable." He worked a bad cramp out of his right arm. "*If* I ever get this stupid assignment done and get my own lamp, that is."

All at once, a prickly, electric buzzing ran up Khalid's spine. His eyes flashed. A joyful grin spread itself wide across his face. There was no mistaking what was happening. Even though the elder genies claimed they could not put the feeling into words, no genie since the dawn of time ever mistook *that* sensation for anything but what it was: Someone was rubbing the lamp.

Khalid straightened his turban, tugged a wrinkle out of his silk trousers, decided he would come out in a puff of blue smoke, then changed his mind and made it orange. The tug of a magical summons drew him from the lamp before he could switch smoke colors a third time. Surrounded by orange clouds, he soared upward. Sunlight from the lamp's spout dazzled his eyes. He burst out into the fresh air with a happy shout, acccompanying his big entrance with a modest thunderclap.

The scrawny, brown-striped alley cat stared up at him and sneezed.

"Hail, O master!" Khalid made his fanciest bow, eyes lowered all the way. It was only good manners. "Name your wish, for I will grant it. Yes, three wishes and no more I will grant you. *However!* not one of these may ask for more wishes. If these terms please you, then by them I am your slave." The last words were uttered in Khalid's deepest voice, for they were the most potent of spells and bound the genie utterly to his newfound master.

The alley cat sneezed again from all the smoke, then rubbed its mangy chin against the lamp again.

Hearing no word from his new master, Khalid looked up. He saw that he was in a dark, smelly, very cluttered place. There were no alleys in the genies' world, nor rubbish heaps, nor cats. The smallest animal Khalid had ever seen was an infant dragon, and that was almost as big as he.

Ah, he thought. *It seems that Tamar was quite right. These mortals* do *come in a bewildering lot of shapes and sizes. This one is a lot smaller than those Master Ishmael showed us in his visions. His whiskers are not as tidy as that General Nahash's, and—What* is *that long thing curled around his feet?*

Khalid squatted down and repeated his offer of three wishes to the cat. He still got no answer and became worried. *Perhaps I should have listened more carefully to what Tamar told me of mortals*, he thought. *The week that Master Ishmael taught about them, I missed class. I vanished so fast during disappearing practice that I made a draft and caught cold from it. I meant to ask Tamar for the lessons, but—*

The alley cat had no idea of the thoughts passing through the young genie's mind. His own mind was full enough, although his stomach was not. He was not a fighter, and he did not find life in the alleys pleasant. Although he could not speak, his heart and mind yearned strongly and constantly for some food, some time to give his fur a proper washing, and a home with someone to love him. He couldn't tell a genie from a human any more than Khalid could tell a human from a cat. Heart full of hope, he went up to Khalid and rubbed against his hands, skinny body shaking with purrs.

"Master?" The genie was bewildered.

"Meow," said the cat.

" 'Meow'," Khalid repeated thoughtfully. "I know I was in class when we learned all the tongues of mortals. That word sounds *almost* Chinese, but the accent is wrong. Hmm. Perhaps this human is like one of those Tamar mentioned— having eyes but unable to see. He cannot speak! And see how he is so weak, he must support himself on all fours, like a unicorn. Oh, Master, Master, if you cannot speak, how can you ever make your wishes? And since I have already bound myself to serving you, how can *I* ever grant them and get out of here?" Feeling very sorry for himself, Khalid sat down cross-legged in the dirty alley while his new master rubbed against him, purring madly.

Without thinking, Khalid let his hand stray to scratch the cat's ears. The purring grew louder and more ecstatic. When the gloomy genie began tickling the cat under his chin while still scratching his ears, something happened.

"Gooooood."

"What did you say, Master?" Khalid dropped his hands and stared.

"More! Don't stop! Grrraaahhh, *more*!"

The demand was inside Khalid's head. The genie laughed, realizing what it meant. "Master, what a fool I am! If you cannot speak with your mouth, I can at least hear your desires with my mind. They teach us that trick when we are babies. Nothing is easier, as long as you *allow* me to read your thoughts. May I—?"

"Scratch under my chin some more before I bite you!"

"At once, O Master." Khalid was his old, smug self again. "I will not even count this as one of your wishes. Speaking of which, what *do* you wish for, Master?"

The thoughts were there almost before Khalid finished the question: "Food. Clean fur. Loving home."

"Hearkening and obedience," said Khalid, doing his best to keep scratching his master's chin. What he wanted to do was leap up and dance with joy. *Three wishes, all so easy, and all made at once! Oh, I'll be in a lamp of my own before another sunset!*

Khalid gestured, and a small banquet was laid before the alley cat. He had read the creature's thoughts and knew what foods would please it most, then he had improved on the order. On a piece of white silk with gold embroidery lay a blue dish filled with tender chicken, skinned and boned, cooked to perfection. Beside it was a red glass bowl of creamy milk, a platter of flaked fish, and some delicately cooked minced beef. There were also six live mice, but they ran off as soon as Khalid materialized them. Face deep in chicken, whiskers dripping milk, the happy cat never missed them.

While the cat ate, Khalid's magic removed all dirt from his fur, mended the patches torn off in fights, cured him of the mange. This done, Khalid searched the neighborhood for the loving home that would fulfill the third wish.

A few blocks away, in the Street of the Fuel Sellers, a young man was walking along very sadly. He was in good health, and neither poor nor ugly, but he was alone. In the same way that the cat's wishes had found their willing way to Khalid's mind, this young man's thoughts were loud and clear for anyone with the power to hear them:

"I'm so lonesome. I wish I had someone—anyone!—to share my home, my life with me."

The young man kicked a piece of broken pottery in the Street of the Fuel Sellers, and before his foot came back to earth he was in the alley. He looked around in confusion, but all he saw was a sleek, pretty cat and some empty dishes on a square of now-dirty white silk. The cat saw his big chance and rushed over to the young man, butting his legs and purring most persuasively.

The lonely young man smiled and picked the cat up. "Well, and what's such a fine-looking fellow like you doing here? You deserve a better home. Would you like to try mine?" The cat almost split himself purring and mewed eagerly. "Fine! It's settled. And these shall be your estate"— he crammed the empty dishes and the silk into the big leather pouch he carried—"for Heaven witness, it's not a rich man's household you're joining."

As he was carrying his new friend from the alley, the young man stumbled over something. Staggering to keep on his feet, he cursed the obstacle until he saw what it was. Still holding the cat, he knelt to pick up the lamp.

"It looks like someone around here has the habit of throwing out pretty things," he told the cat. "A lamp like this and a cat of such beauty in this filthy alleyway . . . It's like something out of those old stories. I wonder—?" The lamp quickly joined the other items in the young man's pouch and he continued to wonder all the way home.

Khalid presented himself before Master Ishmael to make his report.

"So quickly back?" The elder genie sounded pleased, surprised, and doubtful, all at the same time.

"I was fortunate, O Teacher, to find a mortal master whose wishes were simple."

"Truly? Then mortals have changed since my more active days. He did not demand to rule the world? To wed a princess? To wallow in gold?"

"Not at all." Khalid felt only a momentary pang of guilt when he stretched the truth thin by adding, "I believe that the dramatic way I chose to come out of the lamp may have shocked him into keeping his wishes modest."

"My boy!" Ishmael embraced his prize pupil, then invited him to sit down and share some mint tea. "You must tell me the details, and then I shall call the elders together so that we may arrange the ceremony for presenting you with your own lamp."

Khalid sipped his tea and spoke to his teacher as if they were now equals. "I did not have a long time with my first master, but it was still an interesting time. The most difficult part was discovering his wishes."

"So shy? I hope you didn't scare him."

"It was not fear. Poor man, he could not speak. The only sound I heard him make was a queer, rumbly noise, like distant thunder." Khalid tried to mimic a purr.

Ishmael frowned. "Was that—that sound all he could voice?"

"No. There was one other. Very strange it was, and almost like true speech."

"Strange?" The older genie was apprehensive. "How so?"

"I will do my best to imitate it, O Teacher. Bear with me." Khalid concentrated, cleared his throat, and proudly uttered: "Meow."

Ishmael buried his face in his hands and laughed until he cried.

3

"**I** don't see why I have to go through *this* if Master Ishmael thought the whole thing was so cursed funny!" Khalid hunched himself into a new position within his teacher's lamp, but it was just as uncomfortable as the old one. If he had had a hard time finding elbow room in the lamp before, now it was worse. Now he had that awful *book* in there with him.

For what felt like the hundredth time, Khalid slammed the book's cover shut and glared at it furiously. *Yazid's Guide to Better-Known Mortal Animals.* "A child's book, that's what my great and wise teacher, Master Ishmael, gives me to read! 'Study it well,' he says! 'I may choose to give you an examination on your return.' I have never been so insulted. All I needed was for Tamar to find out, or that wooden-headed bully Gamal. A maiden as smart as she is would never want to speak to me again, if she knew what a foolish mistake I made. As for Gamal, he'd laugh himself sick, then run and make sure Tamar heard all about it."

A crick in his neck made Khalid wriggle. One corner of the book jabbed him in the cheek. "Ow!" Grumbling and wishing the book to the eternal fires, Khalid went back to memorizing the chapter on cats while he waited for a second chance at earning a lamp of his own. He was annoyed with his teacher, he was fed up with the world, and he was angry with himself.

Worst of all, he was impatient to find a *real* master,

grant some wishes, and put the whole unpleasant incident of the cat behind him.

"Pick me up, for pity's sake," he muttered, gazing up at the hole at the end of the lamp's spout. "Come on, come on, *find* me, rub me, let me out of here and I'll give you your heart's desire before you can say 'I want it.' Somebody, *any*body, find me! I want to get this stupid test over with so badly, I can taste it. Come on . . ."

He did not understand the dangers of being *too* impatient.

"Well, Boabdil, what do you think? Should I do it?"

The young man looked from the lamp in his hands to the cat at his feet. The cat did not bother to respond. He had been given a nice bowl of milk to drink, a battered old pillow to sleep on, and the freedom to do whatever he liked in his new human's home. He was satisfied, and a satisfied cat never troubles himself about other people's problems. Like all cats, he was a bit of a philosopher. He preferred to think over a problem for a long, long time before doing anything about it. If you thought about some problems long enough, they went away.

"You're not being any help, you know," the young man said, rubbing the cat's neck with his bare toe. He returned his attention to the lamp, took a deep breath, let it out slowly, and said, "At least there's no one but you in the house to see me acting like an idiot, Boabdil."

The cat raised his nose ever so slightly as if to say, *Yes, but cats remember.* It was wasted.

"You know, in the stories, it's always a poor boy who finds the magical lamp and releases the genie," the young man continued. He pushed a lock of straight black hair out of his eyes and rearranged his long, skinny legs on the floor cushion. "Yes, a poor boy or a shipwrecked sailor. Usually the genie who is the Slave of the Lamp brings his master wealth and fame and a beautiful bride. I'd say it was worth the risk of looking like an idiot for the chance of such rewards." He balanced the lamp on the palm of one hand and raised the other, as if about to begin rubbing.

He paused, hit by a second thought. "Sometimes, though, the genie is savage. A monster! No sooner does he emerge from the lamp than he tries to kill the man who freed him." He put the lamp down on the floor beside him and rested his chin in his hand, considering this unhappy possibility.

Now used to regular feedings, the cat Boabdil decided that it was about time for another. His loud meow was supposed to mean "Feed me! NOW!" It wasn't his fault if his human chose to take it for a mystical sign.

"Aha! You are right, Boabdil! In those tales where the genie tried to destroy his master, the man always found a way to trick the creature back into its lamp and toss it to the bottom of the sea. They are remarkably stupid, genies are. I've read all the tales; I know the trick for getting an evil genie to shut himself up in his own lamp. I can control whatever may come out of this one." Full of confidence, he picked up the lamp.

This time he got as far as having his rubbing hand touch its brassy side before he put it down again.

"Do you think *this* genie may have read the same tales I have and be too smart to fall for that old trick, Boabdil?"

Boabdil meowed once more, louder. Having a roof over his head—even such a modest one—had spoiled him already. His life in the alley was not even a bad memory. He knew that as a cat he was entitled to better service than this from his human.

"What is it, Boabdil? Are you angry at me for being a coward?"

"*Mrowrooowwww!*" Frustrated with human stupidity, Boabdil butted his human's hand, hoping the thickheaded two-legs would take the hint and use that hand to fetch an honest cat a nice piece of chicken.

"Ah!" The young man was awestruck. "Behold, a dumb animal pushes my hand closer to the lamp. This is truly a sign from heaven."

Boabdil had his own opinion about who was the dumb one. With nothing but dignity in his stomach, he stalked out of the room. His human did not see him go; he was too busy rubbing the lamp.

Nothing happened, at first. The young man's face fell. "I really am a fool," he mumbled. "Too many days spent listening to the storytellers in the bazaar. My poor dead father was right. No wonder I'm such a sorry excuse for a merchant! The others see me coming and give me poor goods, short prices, and no credit. If I protest, they cover their swindles with long, tearful tales of hungry children and aged parents whom they must support. Even when my common sense tells me they *must* be lying, I wind up believing them every time! Oh, I make it too easy for them, I do. Anyone can cheat a fool."

He was still tearing himself down when he noticed an eyelash-thin wisp of smoke coming out of the lamp's spout. It started off blue, turned orange, then seemed to lose interest in the whole matter of colors and was just a drab, common gray. He took fright and dropped the lamp, but the smoke kept pouring out. Thicker and thicker it grew, until the whole room was filled with a dull haze.

The young man felt panic rising in his chest. He could hardly see in this magically summoned fog, but he was willing to bet that the genie could. (There *had* to be a genie, even if it hadn't materialized yet. As the old saying taught, "Where there's smoke, there are monsters.") If humans had learned the trick of deceiving unfriendly genies, why couldn't genies have learned a trick or two of their own over the years? All this smoke made a perfect ambush. He looked around for the doorway and couldn't find it.

"Help!" he cried. "Someone help me!"

"You're going to have to be more specific than that, you know," said a very cranky voice. " 'Help me' isn't much of a wish. Anyhow, it doesn't count; I haven't offered you anything, yet. O Master." This last was added as an afterthought, with no respect at all.

"Where—?" The young man coughed violently. "Where are you? I can't see a—"

The smoke vanished. The young man found himself eye-to-eye with a being who did not look like any sort of monster. Tall and wide-shouldered, with curly golden-brown hair and bronzed skin, the only thing frightening about him was the ugly sneer twisting his fine-boned face. Apart from the small fortune in jewels sewn to this creature's saffron belt, trimming his blue brocade vest, and pinning the white ostrich plume to his purple turban, the genie could pass for a human being of about his newly made master's age.

It was almost disappointing.

"Are you—are you the Slave of the Lamp?" the young man faltered.

"No, I'm the Giant of the Unclean Dishcloth. Of course I'm the Slave of the Lamp! And who are you?"

The young man knitted his brows. He had heard of genies being eager to please, or sly, or crafty, or downright evil. He had never heard of one being this rude.

Still, nasty or not, the being had come out of the lamp and must possess great magical powers. Better to be polite. He bowed. "O Slave, I am called Haroun ben Hasan, son of Hasan ben Mustapha, a great merchant of this city."

"Great?" There was a positively spiteful tone to the genie's voice now. He looked around the room. It was clean enough, but mostly bare. The cushions were badly worn, the carpet was ragged, the low wooden tables tilted at crazy angles on chipped and broken legs. The genie took it all in, then said, "If this is how the sons of great merchants live, I would hate to see the houses of the poor."

Haroun's black eyes smoldered with anger. "My father *was* a great merchant! His caravans never failed to bring back treasures from the East. Once, this house was filled with music, guests, servants, poetry—"

"I know, I know, and then your evil uncle came along and stole everything. Or the sultan took it. Or maybe the grand vizier felt grabby. I'm not interested. You're wasting your time and mine, crying after what's over and done with, when you could be putting your life back into halfway decent shape. Well? What are you waiting for?"

"Waiting—?"

Khalid made rapid, encouraging motions with his hands. "Come on, hurry it up. You don't *look* like a man who's never read a book in his life. You know what I'm here for or you wouldn't have called me the Slave of the Lamp. Slave—ugh! I hate the word. My name is Khalid. Use it."

"You mean I'm supposed to—you're here to—I can have you grant my wishes?"

23

"Yes, three of them; if you can make them before we both keel over from old age."

"Heaven be thanked!" Haroun clasped his hands together. "I know *exactly* what I want. First, I wish for—"

"Hold it." Khalid held up a delaying finger. "First I have to go through the usual enchanted gibberish binding my magic to your wishes or it's not official and we'll have to waste *more* time while you start all over again. Let's see, how does it go . . . ? Oh, yes. Ahem: Hail O Master name your wish for I will grant it yes three wishes and no more I will grant you if these terms please you then by them I am your slave." He rattled off his speech so swiftly that it seemed like one continuous word. "All right, that's out of the way. Go! And put wings on it, I have better places to be."

"I wish for wealth . . ."

"Granted. I mean, hearkening and obedience." A bag of gold the size of a yearling lion cub fell from the ceiling, nearly smashing Haroun's foot.

"I wish you'd be more careful," Haroun snapped, then clapped his hand over his mouth.

"Too late." Khalid's smile was meaner than a hungry hyena's. The bag of gold jerked itself back up to the ceiling and floated down as carefully as possible.

"I don't think that was fair," Haroun protested.

"I don't have to be fair, I just have to be your slave until you've used up your three wishes. Stop dawdling and try wishing for something useful this time."

"But it *isn't* fair. What I said was just a figure of speech. I shouldn't be punished for a slip of the tongue."

Khalid had a sympathetic nature, but his botched first mission had turned it sour. Ordinarily he would have agreed with Haroun and allowed him to take back the second, wasted wish. He was a generous soul.

However, all he could think of at the moment was what might be happening back in the genie homeland. Time among mortals and time among genies was different. Sometimes days passed back home that were minutes here, and sometimes a single day among the genies turned out to be a mortal century. Where were his classmates? Had Master Ishmael forgotten his promise and told them of

Khalid's blunder? Had Gamal managed to sniff out the truth? Would Tamar still gaze at him as if his smallest magic trick were the cleverest thing she had ever seen? Alone in Master Ishmael's lamp this time, he had had plenty of time to miss the companionship of his class-mates (Gamal excepted) and to notice how the memory that kept returning more than all the rest was a vision of Tamar's face, smiling at him.

He realized that he missed her most of all.

I have to finish this job and get back home, he thought furiously. *I have to speak to Tamar, to tell her my side of what happened, before someone else poisons her mind against me. Why, she might even* laugh *at me! I couldn't stand that. Once I'm back, successful, that first assignment will be nothing more than a joke.*

His impatience to be on his way made Khalid even more irritable. "Whining won't change anything," he told Haroun. "Rules are rules. You know, instead of complaining to me about your own thoughtlessness, you ought to be grateful. I *could* have taken advantage of you when you made your first wish. All you asked for was wealth. You never said how much. Wise wishing is a skill few mortals possess. You have to be spe-ci-fic. I could have given you one gold coin. To a man in your position, that would still be wealth. I think I've been more than kind to you; kinder than you deserve." He folded his arms across his chest and looked haughty.

Haroun looked down at the huge sack of gold. "You're right, I suppose." He sounded glum. "I'm sorry."

"Don't mention it. Next time, think before you speak." Some time passed. Khalid tapped his foot. "You don't need to think *that* long. If you can't think of a third wish, I can make some standard suggestions. We have a nice deal on marriages to the sultan's daughter. Or how about a flying carpet? A palace with invisible servants? A stable of white horses? A palace with invisible servants and a stable full of white horses attached?"

Haroun did not look tempted by any of these. Khalid tried a new tack. "You're a merchant, right? Well, how'd you like a year's supply of whatever kind of bric-a-brac you mortals merch?"

Haroun licked his lip. "I've decided—"

"Good! Come, out with it. What do you want? Speak up!"

"I want . . . I want . . ."

"Yes, yes, yes—?"

"More wishes. As many wishes as there are stars in the heavens and grains of sand on the shore and hairs on all the heads of all the generations of men who have ever been born, and who live now, and who ever will be born, until the end of time." He paused for breath, then added, "Specific enough for you?"

This time the silence was all Khalid's creation.

Finally he said, "Gah."

"What happened to 'hearkening and obedience'?" Haroun wanted to know.

"You can't *do* that! " Khalid exploded.

"Why not? I just did."

"No, I mean you *can't*! It's illegal. You agreed to the terms. Three wishes, no more, and you can't use any of them to wish for more wishes. You *promised*—"

"You never said anything about that; about not wishing for more wishes. Why, it's so simple, I'm surprised no one in the old tales ever thought of it." Haroun straightened his shoulders, pleased with himself.

"I did, too, say something about it! The *However* clause is standard procedure. If it weren't, every genie alive would still be serving his first master. You mortals are such hogs! And no exceptions to the rule, believe me. Even King Solomon couldn't hold on to the genies that served him after they'd done his bidding three times."

"I wish," said Haroun, "you could hear yourself."

"I can hear myself just fine, and I—"

"Not now. *Then.*"

And suddenly Khalid felt a tugging in his chest as his inborn magic stirred. Without his consent, his lips formed the words, "Hearkening and obedience," and the shabby room dissolved into a vision of the same room some minutes earlier. Horror-struck, Khalid saw his own face, bored and arrogant. Here was no honest genie, eager to perform the work of wish-granting for which he had been born. Here was only Khalid the Proud, Khalid the Vain, Khalid whose only care was protecting his own false image as the smartest, the most talented, the best.

He recalled his selfishness and the impatience that gave it birth. He saw that same impatience make him race through the magical words that bound him as Haroun's slave. He heard the words, but more important were the words he did *not* hear.

"The *However* clause!" he cried as the vision vanished. "I forgot the *However* clause!"

It was Haroun's turn to smile. "Careless of you."

Khalid groveled before him and grasped his knees. "O Master! O kind, benevolent, wise Master, you won't make me grant you all those wishes, will you? It wouldn't be fair."

"I don't have to be fair," said Haroun.

"But my forgetting the *However* clause—that was only an accident; a slip of the tongue! Surely I shouldn't be punished for that?"

"Whining won't change anything," Haroun said, enjoying himself more than he'd done in years. "Rules are rules." He patted Khalid on the head, knocking his turban over one eye. "Next time"—he drew out the words on purpose—"*think* before you speak."

Khalid did think. He thought of his past vanity, of Master Ishmael's high hopes, of Gamal's black envy, of the awful, dismal situation into which he'd gotten himself.

He thought of Tamar.

When he had thought enough, he opened his mouth. He didn't speak; he screamed.

"There, there," said Haroun. "Don't make such a fuss. In fact, I *wish* you wouldn't." Against his will, Khalid's screams evaporated. "Much better." Haroun picked up the lantern.

"This is going to be *fun.*"

4

There was a party in the palace that night. There was always a party in the palace.

Rose petals drifted down from the ceiling just as the acrobats finished their famous fifteen-man pyramid in the middle of the feasting hall. The guests applauded wildly and threw handfuls of silver and pearls from the little gold pots their host had provided so thoughtfully. The sight of so much wealth was too much for the men on the bottom row of the pyramid. They lunged forward to gather up as much as they could grab, only to be knocked flat by their fellow performers as the whole carefully balanced arrangement came tumbling down.

The guests applauded louder, laughing. Heartily ashamed of what their greed had done, the acrobats hauled themselves up off each other and slouched out of the hall. A stony-faced servant whose uniform was made from cloth-of-gold gave each of them a small scarlet leather pouch filled with coins as they left. Other servants scurried across the pearl-strewn floor with brooms, sweeping up a fortune that would later be thrown from the highest balcony of the palace to the beggars waiting at the gate below.

In the midst of all this wealth and luxury, the master of the house sat on a gilded throne shaped like a lotus flower. Those guests lucky enough to have been given places near him were beginning to feel the first pangs of hunger. The banquet that came before the entertainment was lavish—the leftovers alone would feed the sultan's harem for a week—but these guests had not eaten a single bite. The roasted peacocks with all their feathers replaced and their toenails painted gold, the broiled doves in plum sauce, the giant carp stuffed with honeyed locusts, all passed them by untasted. The wines of a hundred legendary vineyards were poured into their jeweled goblets, and they left these unsipped.

Those who sat beside the master might feel uncomfortable for an evening, but they would rather starve than risk the alternative. Was it worth taking a mouthful of the most delicious meal ever cooked if the master decided to ask you something *right then*? There you would be, your mouth crammed with a big chunk of coconut cake with apricot glaze, and the master would be staring at you, waiting for a reply.

What if he didn't want to wait? What if waiting made him *angry*? What if the question he had just asked you was something to do with one of his legendary gifts?

My friend, would it please you to have a palace of your own? Oh, nothing fancy. Just a small one, on the shores of a mountain lake; a place to spend the summers. Would you like that?

He had done it before, giving presents so magnificent that some of his guests had fainted when he described them. He was likely to do it again, at any time. It was worth going without dinner when you wanted to keep your mouth ready to say "I accept with thanks, O my lord Haroun ben Hasan!"

This night, though, Lord Haroun did not seem to be his usual, generous self. The most he had given to his guests was a fine silk carpet apiece and pots of costly perfumes to take home to their wives. The guests nearest him noticed how solemn he looked. They did their best to cheer him up, making jokes and singing comical songs for his amusement. Nothing worked. He looked almost as gloomy as that gold-clad servant of his, the one rewarding the entertainers.

Lord Haroun was not amused by the entertainers nor by the songs and jokes of his guests. He stared out over the entire feasting hall and saw nothing. His own dinner, served to him on gem-studded plates, was uneaten. He stroked the brown-striped cat in his lap and fed it the best bits from his platter.

"Well, Boabdil, what do you think?" he asked the animal. "Is this fine? Are you happy?" The cat snorted and dug his claws into his human's satin robes. "Ouch! A little easier there, my friend. If you don't want to answer, I know I can't force you. I only wish—"

The feasting hall froze. The flames of the scented torches stopped burning. The dancing girls stayed where they were, caught in mid-leap. The guests were turned to stone where they sat. Here a goblet hovered an inch away from a thirsty mouth and there a piece of half-chewed food waited to be swallowed.

Only the grim servant in his cloth-of-gold moved. Slowly, wearily, he crossed the floor, weaving his way between the motionless dancing girls. When he reached the foot of Lord Haroun's lotus throne he bowed and said:

"Now what?"

Haroun made a face. "I thought we went over this before, Khalid. That is *not* the way to speak to your Master."

"If it isn't, you only have to *wish* for me to speak to you any way you want," the genie replied. "Why don't you?"

"I don't see why I should waste good wishes on something you can learn to do for yourself perfectly well." Haroun pursed his lips. "You are just like Boabdil; you spend all of your free time looking for new ways to annoy me."

"What free time?" Khalid shot back.

"Oh, never mind." Haroun leaned his cheek on one hand and gestured with the other at the petrified banquet hall. "Look at them," he commanded. "Just look. One hundred fifty of my best friends. How many of them do you think know who I am?"

"The fame of Lord Haroun ben Hasan is greater than that of all the kings, all the princes, all the sultans, all the warriors, all the—"

"Enough!" Haroun cut off Khalid's monotonous recitation. "You know what I mean: How many of them *really* know me? How many would still be my friends if, by some miracle, I awoke tomorrow without the riches your magic has given me and without you to bring me more?"

The genie brightened. "An *excellent* idea, O Master! We ought to try it at once. Now if you'll just be good enough to put that into the form of a wish—"

"You'd like that, wouldn't you?" Haroun gave a dry laugh. "I think that rather than wishing for your magic to abandon me, I shall wish for it to abandon *them* instead. In fact, I *wish* this whole stupid party were over, that my so-called friends were back in their own homes, and that we three were—what was the name of that other palace you conjured up for me? The pinkish one on that quiet street? It had a very pretty garden full of peach trees—"

"The Palace of Eternal Bliss, O Master," Khalid said with a sigh.

"Yes, that's the one. I wish for you to take us there after you've cleared all *this* away." He waved at the frozen banquet.

"Hearkening"—each word was trailed by a sigh—"and obedience."

The frozen torches flickered back to life, but only for a moment. The guests moved again, but not for long. The genie clapped his hands together once, and the lights went out. There was a short explosion of panic-stricken screams from the guests that ended the instant Khalid clapped his hands together a second time. Now total silence matched the total darkness.

"Well?" Haroun's voice came out of the dark. "What's taking you so long? We are waiting."

"Try holding your breath while you wait," Khalid growled, but not loudly enough for his Master to hear. Slowly, reluctantly, he brought his hands together a third time.

The echo of the clap still lingered in Haroun's ears when he and Boabdil found themselves transported to the palace of his wish. They were in the Garden of the Five Tigers, lying on fat silk pillows under the prettiest of the peach trees. Pink and golden fruit hung heavy from the branches. If Haroun wanted to taste the sweetest peaches the world had ever known, he had only to reach up his hand and pick them from where he lay.

Instead he said, "I wish I had a nice peach in my hand right now."

A sigh came from behind the tree trunk. "Hearkening and obedience."

Haroun looked at the peach that had appeared in his hand. He turned it over and around, studying it from every angle. If he had the eyes of a hawk, he would not be able to find any fault with it. In shape, in color, in fragrance, it was entirely perfect. No doubt the first bite he took would prove that its flavor was perfect too.

He did not bother biting it. "You've put the peach in my *left* hand, Khalid," he said. "You know I only use my *right* hand to eat fruit."

Khalid came slouching around the tree to scowl down at his Master. "Your wish didn't say anything about that. You just wished for the peach to be *in your hand.*"

"Yes, but you *know*—"

"I don't know anything!" Khalid bellowed. "Free beings *know* things; slaves just do as they're told. If you want me to show some independent thought, I'll have to *be* independent, and you don't want that, do you?"

Haroun put the peach aside and rubbed his upper lip thoughtfully. "I'm not a fool yet, Khalid. It's not that I don't want you to be free. I have nothing against independence. It's just that when you give most slaves their freedom, they tend to run away with it. That's the part I wouldn't like. I'd miss you."

Khalid plopped himself down in the dewy grass under the peach tree and gave his Master a hard stare. "Maybe if you had some other friends, you wouldn't miss me so much."

Haroun laughed. "I just tried having some other friends, remember? It didn't work." He scratched Boabdil behind the ears. The cat twitched his whiskers at him, sprang up, and stalked away. Haroun called and called after the beast, but Boabdil kept walking until he reached one of the five life-sized onyx tigers that gave this garden its name. Purring, Boabdil leaped into a loop of the sleeping tiger's tail and went to sleep himself.

"You see?" Haroun demanded, gesturing after the cat.

"*That's* independence for you! By my own wish, I commanded you to make that ungrateful animal talk. That way, I thought, I would never lack for a companion. Has he said a single word to me? Does he even appear to understand human speech?"

Khalid gazed after the cat with longing. "There are some things which magic may not change; not even the magic of the world's most powerful genie, and I am certainly not that."

"I wish you were," Haroun said. He was not joking.

"Hearkening," Khalid replied, "but no obedience. It is not possible."

"Why not? Just use your magic—"

"Don't you have ears, O Master? There are always walls, in this world. Some we learn how to go around, or over, or under. Some we learn how to knock down. Some we learn to build doors through. But some things cannot be forced; some things cannot be changed. Eventually we find the wall that stops us, no matter whether we are mortal or magical."

"Very poetical." Haroun knitted his brows. "It still doesn't explain why you can't make a cat speak."

"I made him speak the minute you desired it, O Master," Khalid responded. "What I cannot do is make him want to speak to *you.*"

"What? And why not?"

"Because like all cats, he is an excellent judge of character, and from watching your behavior ever since you got me for your slave, he has come to the conclusion that you are seven kinds of jackass and three sorts of idiot. O Master," he added, trying not to smile.

Haroun's stormy face grew darker. "I don't believe it. I *refuse* to believe it. You are using my poor, innocent cat as an excuse for your haphazard magic. The best genies can use their powers to do anything! I know; I've read the old tales."

"Have you? I cannot remember the last time I saw you pick up a book, O Master."

"I've been—I've been busy." Haroun shifted uncomfortably. The truth is often itchier than a swarm of red ants. "And anyway, it's none of your business!" he lashed out.

"No? Then what is my business, O Master? I'm sure you'll tell me."

"I'm still waiting for that peach! In the *proper* hand, this time."

Khalid did nothing. He did it in a way guaranteed to enrage Haroun.

"Well?" the young man snapped. "Where is it? I *said* I was waiting."

"So am I." The genie had come to treasure every tiny chance he got to slip little burrs into his Master's cushiony life.

Haroun gritted his teeth. "Very well. I *wish* I had a nice, plump, delicious, edible peach from one of these trees in my *right* hand now."

"Hearkening and obedience." The peach appeared.

Haroun sniffed it. He was always extra careful about Khalid's gifts immediately after one of these Master/genie discussions. Bickering gave him an appetite, and once he had wished for a fine quail dinner. The dinner Khalid produced, like the peach, was perfect. It even *smelled* perfect. Haroun had picked up one of the birds and taken a tremendous bite . . .

. . . of the most perfect wooden quail he'd ever tasted.

It didn't matter how real this peach smelled; Haroun had learned that lesson from the wooden quail. Very cautiously, he set his teeth to the velvet skin and took a tentative nibble. Sweet juice filled his mouth.

"Will that be all, O Master?"

"Mmmm?" Haroun was so happy with the delectable peach that Khalid had to repeat the question. "Oh, yes, yes, that's all for now. You may go."

"Ahem."

"I mean, I *wish* you would go away—"

"Hearkening and—"

"—to whichever room of *this palace* you like!" Haroun winked. "You don't escape me that easily. Nor will you escape until my wishes run out or else I decide I've had enough of wishing."

"Until you've had enough?" Khalid groaned. "Why not just say *until the world's end* and be honest about it?" He did not whisk himself out of the Garden of the Five Tigers, but straggled off into the palace, dragging his feet.

Haroun shook his head. "Tsk. To hear him carry on, you'd think I was one of those really greedy people. Of course I'll have enough of wishing someday. Only not just yet. In fact"—he pulled himself up straighter on his pillows and looked self-righteous—"he ought to appreciate me more. If I freed him, he'd only fall into the hands of another person, and *that* one would probably be greedy enough for twelve misers and a tax collector. I'm doing him a favor, keeping him here serving me. Is he thankful? No more than that miserable cat of mine."

Still licking peach juice from his fingers, Haroun continued to marvel over the ingratitude of cats and genies. He did not see Boabdil rouse himself, leap down from the sleeping tiger statue, and run into the palace.

Far above the Garden of the Five Tigers, the ungrateful cat sat on a windowsill and spoke to the equally ungrateful genie: "No luck."

Khalid slumped into a chair beside the arched window and closed his eyes. "I had hoped"—

—"that I would be the key to free you?" Boabdil switched his tail. "You expect too much. I'm just a cat."

"But I was kind to you! In all the old tales, when the hero is kind to an animal, that animal always finds a way to pay him back when he's in trouble."

"I think you've spent too many hours with your eyes in a book and not enough reading the world. My human does that, too. I'm surprised the two of you don't get along better; you have much foolishness in common." He paced the windowsill, tail high. "Tales or no tales, I don't know why you come to me for ideas of how to get you out of this fix."

"Cats are wise."

"Wise enough not to get ourselves into predicaments like yours in the first place. Therefore we have no experience with getting *out* of them." Boabdil settled down in the sunniest spot on the sill and closed his eyes. "I'm going to nap now. Scat!"

Shoulders bent with all the misery in the world, Khalid

rose to go. He lingered awhile to gaze enviously at the cat on the windowsill. A full belly, a clean coat, and another living soul to care for him: that was happiness. It didn't require palaces or performers, gold platters or gemmed goblets. Food, comfort, love: Why couldn't Haroun learn that simple lesson and be content?

"He never will," Khalid said softly to himself. "He will continue to crack his brain and my back trying to come up with the perfect wish to bring him happiness. We shall grow old together, until he dies with ten thousand times ten thousand unused wishes still owing him. And in all that time, my classmates will have served hundreds of masters. They will learn, they will grow, they will become the respected elders of our people, they will teach a new generation of genies!"

Tears blurred his sight. He had a vision of his old, beloved classroom full of strange, young faces. He saw himself come in—a worn and weary self who came to tell Master Ishmael that after so-and-so many mortal years, he had *finally* fulfilled his first mission.

Master Ishmael was not there. Gamal had taken his teacher's place. The other genie's lip curled in scorn when he saw Khalid standing alone in the doorway. *What! Forgotten how to materialize! And you used to be so good at it, Khalid!* Every word cut like a dagger.

But that was not the worst of it. She was there, too: Tamar. She sat on her familiar carpet and looked just as beautiful as the last time he'd seen her. He tried to make her look at him. She saw him, but it was the same way she saw a wall, or a door, or a table; there was no recognition.

Then he realized that she was at the head of the class, too, her carpet floating beside Gamal's. Gamal reached out and took her hand. *Too late, Khalid,* he sneered. *Too bad.*

Khalid saw himself rushing up the aisle, jostling the carpets to either side. *Tamar! Tamar!* He called her name again and again; she did not hear. *Tamar!* He was shouting now. *Tamar, you have to hear me! Tamar!*

"Tamar!"

Khalid was at the window without knowing how he'd

gotten there, leaning out over the street. His fingernails dug into the soft pink plaster on the outside of the palace wall.

"Hey! Be careful!" Boabdil leaped up, fur bristling, and jumped for the safety of the room. "You almost knocked me overboard," he accused Khalid.

Khalid ignored him. In the street below, a face was turned up toward the palace, toward this very window. It was a face that was dear to Khalid—dear too late, he'd thought—a face that was first bewildered, then astonished, then lit up with the loveliest of smiles. She was dressed in the plain garb of a common mortal woman, a market basket on one arm. Already it was half-full of a variety of fruits from a merchant's stall.

"Tamar!"

"Ten thousand devils seize your tongue, you impudent rogue!" cried the merchant, shaking his fist at Khalid. "I will not have you bothering my customers! This is a respectable woman—even if she is robbing me blind by the minute. How dare you shout at her?"

Tamar was giggling. "Good merchant," she said, "it's all right. That is an old friend of mine." Tilting her head and waving, she shouted back, "Khalid!"

The merchant was aghast. "Such behavior! For a woman to act so is scandalous, scandalous. If you do not care about your reputation, think of mine! Be gone! Be gone before you cause me to lose all of my customers!"

Tamar became suddenly serious. "Is that what you desire, Merchant?" she asked.

He crossed his arms. "I do."

"Is it what you want?"

"It is."

"But is it—is it what you *wish*?"

"Yes and indeed and truly!"

She pressed her hands together. "Hearkening and obedience." She vanished, leaving him to gape at the place on the street she had left empty and the market basket she had left him full of coins.

5

Tamar hugged her knees to her chest and giggled. "Just look at that poor man, Khalid," she said in a whisper, peering cautiously out of the window. "Look, but don't let him see you looking. Did you ever see such an expression? Misery is spelled out across his face in letters a foot high. Now he realizes that the shameless woman he was so angry with is really a shameless genie. A genie that granted him one wish, out of the kindness of her heart, and he wasted it on wishing her away! Yet see. Now he counts the basketful of coins I left him and knows that in spite of his wasted wish, he has come out of this pretty well. He's starting to smile. No, no! Now he's remembering the wasted wish and back comes the long face. Oh, aren't mortals funny?"

"Hilarious." Khalid did his best to share in Tamar's amusement, but he felt more like sympathizing with the bamboozled merchant. He knew how badly it hurt to be hooked on the wrong end of magic.

Tamar continued to spy on the merchant from her comfortable perch. The window she had chosen for her pryings had a wide sill, well padded to make a snug seat. "Do you think he'll ever decide whether to be happy or sad?"

"I expect he'll either make up his mind one way or the other, or else he'll break his neck trying to skip with joy and kick himself at the same time." Seated cross-legged in mid-air, Khalid made an impatient gesture and a refreshment tray materialized before him. Another flick of his fingers and the brass teapot lifted itself to pour steaming hot mint tea into a pair of earless, leather-wrapped cups.

Something disturbing in Khalid's voice made Tamar suddenly lose interest in her merchant. Concerned, she asked, "Is everything well with you, Khalid?"

"Oh, very well." He wiggled one finger, and the little silver dish of honey tilted a thin, golden stream into his cup and hers. The tea stirred itself without benefit of spoon, churning up a thick froth of rainbow bubbles on the surface of each cup. He floated one across to her. "And you?"

"I can't complain." She took her cup and sipped it. "I've earned a lamp of my own at last, and I can't say I'm not glad. Do you know how cramped you get in one of those enchanted rings? That was my first assignment: a ring. From there I worked my way up to a magic bracelet, then an emerald-studded belt, then a brass bottle, and just when I'd given up all hope, the Council of Elders said I was ready for the real thing. At last! It's a very nice lamp." A coy note came into her voice. "Perhaps you'd like to come up and see it sometime?"

Khalid's throat tightened. The joy he'd first felt at seeing Tamar again had evaporated. Having her here only increased his pain.

Look at her, he thought. Listen to her, chirping merrily away about all her different assignments, all the mortals she's served. She hasn't any idea about the awful mess I've gotten myself into. She doesn't know that she's visiting a prisoner.

With all his heart he yearned to seize Tamar's hand, to leap with her out the window, to fly away to wherever she desired—even to that pretty little lamp of hers, the one she spoke of so proudly! He knew that he could not; that maybe he could never.

She mustn't know, he decided firmly. *She wouldn't laugh at me—not Tamar—but she'd feel sorry. I don't want her pity. Better to send her away from here thinking I'm still the self-centered snob I always was in class. Better to have her remember me as a braggart than as a fool.*

Very deliberately, he yawned in Tamar's face. "Maybe

someday I will pop by that little lamp of yours. If I haven't got anything better to do. I'm a very busy genie."

"I know."

His brows went up sharply in alarm.

"I mean," she added, "that's what everyone back home assumed when you didn't come back for graduation. We were all so proud of you!"

Khalid breathed easier. Relieved, he could not keep from teasing, "All?"

Tamar shrugged prettily. "I can work the seven hundred and seventy-seven greater magics, but when it comes to Gamal, even I don't expect miracles." A look of distaste flitted over her face. "When I was still in that enchanted ring, he had the nerve to barge in and suggest we share it as a married pair. The idea! It wasn't even an engagement ring."

Khalid tried his utmost to appear indifferent to what Tamar was telling him, but his flesh went cold at the thought of Gamal anywhere near Tamar. "Master Ishmael put him in his place when you told him about that incident, I'm sure," he drawled.

"Master Ishmael is gone."

It was no use trying to pretend disinterest. Khalid was not that good an actor. "Gone? Gone how? Where?"

"No one knows." Tamar's eyes grew shiny with tears. "It was shortly after you left us. The Council of Elders summoned him and he never came back. We had a new teacher the next day, a scrawny old thing with breath like a dead goat and no more common sense than a clay jug. He thought he was magic's gift to the world, though, and Gamal was right there to agree with him all the way. I knew Gamal was a bully, but I never imagined he could be such a weasel-faced flatterer, too." She turned grim. "Flattery pays. Our noble teacher saw to it that Gamal was assigned to a lamp right away. No rings or bracelets or brass bottles for his pet, oh no!"

"With a lamp of his own, at least he won't trouble you any further," Khalid said, trying to sound casual about it.

"You think so?" Tamar's sparkling eyes darkened. "Ha! Beggars have fleas that are easier to get rid of than Gamal. He cheats, did you know that? Mortals are fair game for trickery, but all in the spirit of fun. He treats his as cruelly as he can without attracting the unfavorable attention of the Council of Elders.''

"How do you know this?"

"He brags about it!" Tamar took short, angry sips from her cup. "Every time he finishes with one master, he rushes off to find me and crow over how badly he fooled the poor, idiotic mortal. Oh, Khalid, our purpose in this life is to share our magical powers with mortals. The more mortal masters we serve, the greater our own ability to work magic grows!"

"Practice makes perfect, as Master Ishmael used to say," Khalid recited dully. His own tea lay untasted in his hand. "And by giving, we receive."

The ancient lessons hung heavy in his heart. Serving only one master, he had gained experience, but not ability. A genie's magic was like the never-empty wine jug in the old story: the more it was passed around, the more wine flowed freely back into it. Yet if it only sat untouched in a corner, the sun and the air itself would cause the wine within to evaporate until one day its selfish owner came to find it truly empty once and for all.

"But that's it, Khalid; Gamal doesn't give. Not really. He always finds the means to grant his master's wish so that the result is unbearable. If a man asks for wealth, he receives stone coins the size of millstones. Wealth, yes, from an island over the edge of the world! If a woman asks for beauty all men may admire, Gamal transforms her—into the swiftest and sleekest of racehorses!"

"Sneaky," Khalid said, pretending to be shocked. Actually he was busy making mental notes to apply Gamal's methods to Lord Haroun.

Then Tamar said, "In all the time you have been gone, with all the masters you must have served, I know that you never once behaved so wickedly as Gamal."

Khalid's mental notes puffed themselves up like a balloon and popped. He felt his cheeks turn hot with a guilty blush. "Of course not," he mumbled. "Never."

"Oh, let's forget about Gamal!" Tamar made a graceful gesture that beckoned the teapot over to refill her cup. Another wiggle of her slim fingers caused an almond cake to float from the platter into her waiting hand. "It's news of your life that I'm famished for, Khalid. The adventures you must have had by now! The grand variety of human masters you must have served! Were any of them kings or princes? Did you ever appear to a poor beggar boy and make him into a great lord, with a beautiful princess for a wife? Have you ever met a mortal poet, or taught new tales to a storyteller?"

Khalid made himself chuckle, although his heart wasn't in it. "Why don't you ask me whether I ever obeyed the beautiful princess?"

Tamar did not find this thought at all funny. Her sweet mouth pulled itself tight as a drawstring purse. "Really, Khalid, even I know that beautiful princesses are kept locked away in their fathers' palaces. How would one of them ever get her hands on a filthy old lamp?"

"Well, my lamp could have been found in the street by a beggar girl, and she might've wished to become a beautiful princess." Khalid was beginning to enjoy this.

Tamar wasn't. "Then she would be a fool! Who would want to wish for a life you spend shut up all day, even if you are shut up in a palace?"

"Then she could wish for me to stay and keep her company," Khalid suggested, his faint, teasing smile now genuine.

"Ohhh!" With an impatient sound, Tamar leaped to her feet and brushed cake crumbs from her robes. "You are the most infuriating genie I ever knew! Next you'll be telling me that old story about how the beauty of mortal women is so much more wonderful than the beauty of female genies because you know it must fade away one day. Well? Why not say it?"

He studied her as she stood there, eyes bright, chin raised, defying him, and his heart ached. He could not tease her any longer. Instead he rose from his invisible seat and took her hands in his own. "I can't say it," he said.

"Why not?"

"Because it would be the last of too many lies."

He would have said more, but just then there was a terrible racket from the hallway. The cat Boabdil came bounding into the room, every wisp of fur on his back standing straight up, his tail puffed out like a feather duster. "Brace yourself," he announced. "Here he comes with another bee in his turban—no, a whole swarm of them!" He was followed a moment later by Haroun.

Khalid's Master was a sight to behold. His gorgeous silken clothing was torn in a score of places and he was covered head to foot with white plaster dust, gray-green smears of mildew, and yards of cobwebs. He was coughing badly with every step he took. At the sight of him, Tamar veiled herself and drew back into the darkest corner of the window seat.

In his hands, Haroun held a gigantic book. It was so large, his knees buckled under the weight of it. It was as big as the back of the king's second-best throne, and as thick as the cushion on the seat of that same piece of royal furniture. Its cover was fine old leather, dyed red and bound with an iron spine, corners, and a heavy latch. There were still a few glimmering flakes of gold clinging to the binding to show that the heavier metal had once been richly gilded.

"Khalid!" Haroun called, squirming as he tried to wipe himself clean of dust on his shoulders. "Khalid, I have found it! I've found the answer to what I most want in the world!" He coughed some more and sneezed seven times in a row. "Khalid, I—oh, bother. I wish I could see clearly."

"Hearkening and obedience."

The dust and dirt peeled away from Haroun's body like a white sheet and blew out the window.

"That's better. Now I wish you'd bring me a table, so I could put this thing down." Haroun was so overcome with the burden of the book that he did not notice Tamar there, at first.

"Hearkening and obedience," Khalid repeated, his voice flat. A suitable table appeared. He kept his eyes fixed on it, even though it was a common table like a thousand others. He did not want to look at Tamar. He knew that she could count up to three, and any moment now . . .

"That's better." Haroun let the book drop with a loud thud. He cleared his throat a few more times before saying, "This dust is terrible! I wish I had a nice, cool drink of pomegranate juice."

"In which hand, O Master?" Khalid stalled uselessly.

"Oh, any one you like; I don't care! And if you'll stop those silly little games about fulfilling my wishes to the letter, I promise not to act like a spoiled infant over which of my hands you put things in. This"—he smacked the book, sending up further clouds of dust—"has made me realize what is truly important for my happiness; and it's not having peaches pop up in one hand instead of the other. Well, Khalid? Why are you waiting? I did say I wish . . ."

"Hearkening"—even though Khalid was not looking at her, he knew that behind his back, Tamar's eyes were growing wide with horror and realization—"and obedience."

A silver goblet of ice-cold pomegranate juice appeared in Haroun's hand, its sweet-tart aroma so tempting the parched young man smacked his lips in anticipation. Just as he raised it to his lips, Tamar cried:

"Name of ten thousand demons, what kind of crazy mortal is this?" Her exclamation startled Haroun badly. Juice spritzed everywhere. "Three wishes!" the female genie went on. "Three wishes tossed away on the most trivial of desires—to clear off some dust, to fetch a table, to bring him a drink—and yet he stands there, sipping pomegranate juice as if magic were as common to him as old rags. Oh, my poor Khalid"—she ran to his side and threw her arms around his neck—"how awful for you to serve a madman! How happy you must be that at least it was over quickly. Come with me, now, and we'll see if we can't put your lamp in the path of a sane master this time."

Khalid stayed where he was, eyes on the floor. Tamar might as well have hugged a post. Haroun was still sputtering, his face and clothing dripping with the scarlet juice. "I wish—" Haroun began. "I wish only in a manner of speaking that you would ask my permission before you have visitors, Khalid. And I really wish I were dry and had fresh clothes on."

This time, Khalid's "Hearkening and obedience" was said as if it were something shameful. In the beat of a moth's wing, Haroun was wearing a completely new set of gorgeous white silk robes trimmed with gold and turquoise. His face

45

was also dry, and with the pomegranate juice cleared from his eyes, he got his first good look at Tamar.

He forgot all about the pomegranate juice. He forgot all about the book. A slow smile stretched the corners of his lips until they seemed ready to touch his ears.

"Well, well, well. If you are the sort of guest who comes to see Khalid, forget what I said about no visitors." He made her his most elegant bow. "I am Lord Haroun ben Hasan, at your service, Fair One. And what sort of enchanted garden grew a flower so beautiful as you?"

Tamar was not smiling. "Four," she said.

Haroun cocked his head to one side. "I beg your pardon?"

"That was four wishes. I can count. And Khalid granted them all."

"Of course; why not? He's a genie. Genies do that sort of thing every day. My dear, haven't you heard any of the old stories?"

"Yes, but four wishes—!" Tamar was insistent that Haroun understand how improper it all was.

"Closer to four hundred," Khalid said, in a voice as cheerful as the bottom of a dry well. "Or four thousand. Not that it matters."

Tamar looked sharply from Haroun to Khalid and back. Her brow was heavily creased in thought. "Either you are mad," she said, pointing at Haroun, "or you have lost your mind"—this time she pointed at Khalid—"or I have been working too hard and I need a vacation."

"Good idea," Khalid said. "Leave now."

"I won't hear of it!" Haroun continued to waste his most charming smiles on the female genie. "My rose, you are the answer to the very wish I was about to make. Behold."

Gently he steered her away from Khalid and over to the table where the massive book lay. Taking care, on account of the dust, he opened it to a page marked with a wide piece of scarlet ribbon. "Before your friend Khalid and I began our—ahem—business arrangement, all that was left me in this world was a trunk filled with my father's dearest possessions."

"Were you a beggar boy, then?" Tamar asked.

"No, but I wasn't far from it. Oh, it was a lucky day for me when I found Khalid's lamp! Why, it seems like yesterday."

"Wasn't it?"

Haroun laughed. "If yesterday were almost a year ago, yes. However, this book is none of our friend Khalid's doing. It was my father's, and I found it just now, at the bottom of that trunk I mentioned. I was so bored, you see. It's not easy, deciding what to wish for next. At first I thought I'd ask him to make me Supreme Ruler of the World, but then I recalled we'd tried that for my birthday and I didn't like it. While I was wandering around the palace, trying to come up with an idea for a wish, I stumbled across my father's trunk. Perhaps I'd find something in it that would inspire me, I thought, and so I opened it, found this book, and now all my problems are about to be solved forever! Why, if this wish turns out as well as I hope, it might even mean that I won't need Khalid around anymore."

"But after three wishes he's not supposed to—"

Haroun did not hear her. He was running his finger across the old, old words on the page he had marked. "There it is! Can you read? It's so simple, really. Here I've been racing after happiness in a dozen different shapes, and the key to it lies in a single phrase."

Tamar bent forward to read the words Haroun's finger underlined. Khalid remained where he was, downcast, seemingly forgotten by the two of them. " '. . . for the garden of joy lies open to the man who finds the gate, and a wise man knows that the gate opens at the touch of love.' " She looked up at Haroun, and suddenly she knew why he was gazing at her with that empty-skulled grin.

"Yes," he said, clasping her hands. "The touch of love: to be adored forever by a suitably beautiful wife. That would make me happy, and so that is what I'll wish for."

"A princess, I suppose," Tamar said.

"Hmm? No, no. I was going to wish for a princess, but Khalid might act up and bring me an ugly one. It's easier to wish for him to turn you into a princess after we're married."

Tamar did not try to pull her hands away; not yet. "Don't you think there's something you should ask me first, before you go wishing me turned into a princess?"

"Like what? Oh, do you mean you might not want to be a princess? Well, if you insist, I could live with that. I may even give you three of my wishes as a wedding present. Won't that be nice?"

"Wonderful." Tamar's eyes were hard and cold as marbles. Khalid remembered her temper from class, and he didn't like the approaching-thunderstorm sound of her voice.

He hurried over to lay his hands on her shoulders. "Tamar, whatever you're thinking of doing to him, don't! He's my Master! Unless he's the one who starts the fight, I must protect him against all magical attacks until he has used up the wishes I still owe him. Please, I don't want to fight you."

When Tamar turned her face toward Khalid, it looked as smooth and white as an egg, but the sight of it left him feeling as if this egg were about to crack wide open and hatch a fire-breathing dragon any minute. "I can wait," she said. "I'm perfectly willing to wait until he's used up all the wishes you owe him. And do you know why I'm willing to wait? I'll do it because right now, there isn't anything on this world or under it I want half so much as to give this clown a good, firm, healthy kick to the moon!"

Khalid turned pale. Meanwhile, Haroun tried to get Tamar to pay attention to him again. "My pearl," he said, "I think I'll have to wish you become a princess after all. Princesses never talk like that about their husbands. Khalid, listen carefully: I wish to marry this girl at once!"

"Hearkening . . ."

6

"**W**ell, you don't need to sulk about it."

Tamar lay on her belly on a small yet elegant flying carpet, blue and red with silver tassels. Fortunately the ceilings in Haroun's palace were high enough to allow her to hover a good ten feet above his head. From the expression on his face, he looked ready to start throwing things at her any moment.

"It's not fair!" he shouted. "You're a genie, too!"

"What's not fair about that?" Tamar wanted to know. "It's an odd job, but somebody's got to do it." She caused a bowl of salted almonds to appear and dropped them onto Haroun's head, one by one.

Khalid was quick to materialize a parasol over his angry Master. The falling almonds made a gentle pit-a-pat sound, like rain. The cat Boabdil came in to see what all the yelling was about. He batted at the nuts with his paws.

"Tamar, please . . ." Khalid's eyes begged her to stop teasing the young mortal.

"No, I won't!" she replied to his unspoken request. "I think he's been awful, treating you like this, and he deserves whatever little annoyances I can dish out. You are a disgrace to mortals everywhere, Haroun! You ought to be ashamed of yourself. You don't have to be so greedy. Most people are more than happy to have three wishes granted; even one! I admit, Khalid made a mistake, but why couldn't you just take fifty wishes—or a hundred, if you had to have them—

and then let him go?" Small lightnings flashed from her eyes. "You are worse than Gamal."

She made a beehive grow from the roof and filled it with furious bees, then changed the falling almonds to honey drops.

"Tamar, he's not really that bad," Khalid protested. He summoned up a great wind that blew bees, hive, honey, and all out the window and over the city rooftops.

"You have to say that. He's your Master."

"Yes, but it's still the truth."

She remained unsatisfied. "Prove it!"

"I can't." Khalid looked down. "I just feel it."

"If he's so wonderful, why won't he set you free?"

Khalid opened his mouth to speak, then closed it when he didn't have an answer for her.

Tamar folded her arms. "I thought so."

"That's not fair, either," Haroun objected. "I am going to release Khalid . . . someday."

"When?" Tamar pressed the point.

Haroun looked like a small boy who has been caught stealing cake. "I said when. Someday. Someday when"—he gave the matter a lot of thought—"when I'm perfectly happy."

Tamar rolled over on her carpet with a loud moan. "Powers that be! Have I heard right? Oh, poor Khalid, if all your mortal master wants is not mere happiness, but perfect happiness, then you are doomed!" She turned over again and gave Haroun a piercing frown. "But if you are doomed, I shall see to it that you're not the only one."

Haroun licked his lips nervously. "Does she mean me?" he asked his genie. Khalid just shrugged. This was not a good enough reply for Haroun's liking. He grew angry.

"You'd better not try anything!" he shouted at Tamar. "In fact, I *wish* you would never do anything to harm me."

There was a silence in the room. Scowling in earnest now, Haroun turned to Khalid and demanded, "*Well!* Isn't this the time for you to say 'Hearkening and obedience'?"

"Master, I can say it until I am blue in the face, for all the good it will do. I can protect you if Tamar uses her magic to attack you directly—indeed, I *must* do so—but I cannot

51

use my powers to block those of another genie. That is impossible. Your wish must remain ungranted."

"And I'm not fool enough to attack you directly," Tamar informed Haroun, a disconcerting half-smile playing about her lips. "But have you ever thought about how many times and places there are in a day for *little* things to go wrong?"

She half closed her eyes and began to count off the possibilities on her fingers: "Hot bathwater that suddenly turns to ice. Delicious foods that attract every insect in the city the moment before you try to take a bite. Fine carpets that hump up under your feet without warning and make you crash down flat on your face. Sweet dreams that are abruptly interrupted by nightmares of the most hideous terror. Why, I can think of one hundred thousand and seventy-three creative uses for fleas alone, right off the top of my head. Shall I go on?"

"Don't bother. I understand you." Haroun had gone from looking guilty to looking sullen. "Now you listen to *me*. For every pebble you place under my feet, I can make your friend Khalid move boulders. For every feast of mine you spoil, Khalid will be commanded to conjure up a hundred more. Do you want to make my life a series of burrs, fidgets, and itches, just to see how long it takes before I give in? Well, *I* want to see how much magic a genie can spend on one Master before he uses himself up altogether and blows away!"

Tamar went white. "You wouldn't."

"Not if *you* won't." Haroun grinned, the winner.

"You are horrible! Unspeakable! Hateful!"

"And safe from you." He winked at her. It was the last straw.

"Oooooohhhhhhhh!" With a terrible growl, Tamar vanished. Khalid stood staring mournfully at the empty air where she had floated.

"Snap out of that," Haroun ordered, nudging the genie with his elbow. "She's gone; think no more of her. I have work for you to do."

"Yes, Master." Boiled cabbage had more life to it than Khalid.

"Here, now! Perk up! I meant what I said about freeing

you. You will be free once I say I've wished my last wish, won't you?"

"I suppose." Khalid remained glum.

Haroun really threw himself into trying to jolly up the disconsolate genie. "Well, so I shall! And it won't take forever, either. You see, thanks to that wonderful book my father left me, I know the one thing I need for perfect happiness."

"Yes. A bride. I'm sure that once you are married, you will be perfectly happy. Perfectly." The genie did not sound convinced, nor did he care what he sounded like. "I'll just go and fetch you one, then. What size?" If Khalid's lower lip had drooped any further, it would have swept the floor.

Haroun clicked his tongue. "No, no, no. You can't just order brides as if they were sugarplums. Love is somewhat different from shopping. I must have a bride worthy of me, certainly: young, beautiful, the daughter of a king! But she must love me—love me not because I am Lord Haroun, master of great wealth and commander of an actual genie, but because—can you guess why?" He gave Khalid a foxy look.

"I don't know." The genie slumped cross-legged to the floor and rested his face on one fist. "Why should she?"

"Because I am *me*, of course!"

"Oh. That." In a softer voice Khalid added, "I'll be stuck working for this one for a hundred years."

"I hope you don't mind?"

"Not at all. Plenty of room."

"Thank you. You're very kind."

"My pleasure." The cat Boabdil thought a friendly purr at the magical being who had entered his body. Although he could not smell her properly—she being inside him and all—he could use the far keener sense—the *hrrown*, or Nose of the Mind, as cats everywhere called it—to decide that she was acceptable. Not a cat, but almost as good.

"Did you hear what that idiot just said?" Tamar demanded.

"How could I not?" Boabdil sent her a feline chuckle. "You heard it with my own ears."

"Loved for himself! By a princess, no less! There's as

much chance of that as of a cobra being loved for his winning smile.''

"So you think it's impossible?'' the cat asked.

"It would have to improve to be impossible!''

"Then I suggest you think of a way to improve it. Look.'' Boabdil cocked his head so that Tamar could see Khalid, crumpled up, his head cradled on his updrawn knees.

The cat felt her sob. "Oh, my poor darling!'' The thought of her tears washed over Boabdil's mind like a cold, gray rain. He fluffed out his fur, irritated.

"Mewling like a hungry kitten won't help him. Come along with me.'' Tail high and proud, the cat stalked from the room.

"Wait! Please, wait. What are you doing? Where are we going?'' Tamar begged.

"Where?'' The thought was as scornful as any cat worth his whiskers could take it. "Not to sea, certainly, nor into the desert. Where do you think we're going? We go to the king's palace, and we will not come back here without a royal bride!''

7

Very gently, trying to be a polite and thoughtful guest, Tamar made Boabdil lift his head so she could see the walls of the king's palace.

"It isn't much of a palace," she commented.

"He isn't much of a king," the cat replied.

Boabdil sniffed at the crumbly yellow stones of the palace's outer wall. The walls were extremely old, and many a young urchin of the streets had managed to scrawl his name or a nasty picture on them with charcoal.

"Disgraceful!" Tamar exclaimed.

"Perhaps the king does not have enough money or enough men to scrub his walls again," the cat suggested. "I must say, my human has more than one palace and he manages to keep all of them spotless, inside and out."

"Your human has help," Tamar said bitterly.

"Not for long." Boabdil smirked. "There's the gate. Let's go and find our princess."

He trotted off briskly. For Tamar, being inside the cat was even worse than being cramped up in her first enchanted ring. Whenever the cat moved, she got a terrible shaking. The lurch she'd felt when Boabdil leaped from Haroun's palace window still made her stomach tremble. She could have made herself more comfortable, but she was afraid of bumping into the wrong things and doing some damage.

Everything is so dark in here! I guess this must be part of what makes cats so mysterious, she thought to herself. *Even they don't know why they do some things.*

As her eyes grew used to the shadows, she saw that Boabdil's mind was a neat and orderly collection of many lidded baskets. The two biggest she could see were labeled FOOD and COMFORT. There were others, almost as big, marked HOME, FREEDOM, HUNTING, LADY CATS, and THE MOON. She reached out to shift her weight carefully and felt something small under her hand. Picking it up and bringing it close to her eyes, she saw that it was a basket no bigger than a walnut. The label on it read: THE IMPORTANCE OF WHAT HUMANS THINK OF CATS.

The cat stopped without warning and Tamar fell against a stack of medium-sized baskets. "Oh, I'm sorry." she cried, hurrying to put them back in order. "I hope I haven't harmed anything."

"Think nothing of it," the cat answered. "You didn't even hurt my feelings."

"Where are we?"

"The great gate. Can you see all right?"

Tamar moved so that she could use Boabdil's eyes. Though the wall itself was not much, the gate was tremendous. Up and up it rose in a pointed arch. Blue and green and gold tiles decorated it in wavy patterns, until it looked like the entrance to a wonderful undersea land. The huge iron grille used to lock the gate in times of war was wide open. Tamar saw a moving forest of human legs rushing in and out before her. All at once a great cry rang out and the legs ran even faster, to get out of the way of a set of galloping hooves. The horse raced past, kicking up a dust cloud that made Boabdil sneeze and toss Tamar back and forth inside him.

"The way is open. We are in luck," the cat said. "What shall I do?"

"Go in. Follow the tracks of that horse. No one comes riding so fast unless he bears an important message, and all important messages go straight to the king. Once we find the king, it will be simple to find any spare daughters he may have hanging around the palace."

"If you say so." Obediently, Boabdil set off the way the horse had gone.

Tamar's theory proved right. They traced the horse to

the royal stables. From there, the genie told the cat to use his magnificent gift of smell to follow the rider who had dismounted from the horse. The trail led up a wide flight of dirty white steps, down a towering hall lined with sick-looking potted palm trees, through a courtyard where all the fish in a scummy ornamental pond and half the rose-bushes surrounding it had died, and finally into a small, dingy, stale-smelling room. At every step Tamar advised Boabdil to hide wherever he could, and where he could not hide to walk close to the wall. It would not do to be discovered.

In this room, however, there was no choice. There was nowhere to hide, and the walls were all lined with heavy bookshelves. Boabdil was clean, as all cats like to keep themselves, and his shiny fur stood out like a lighthouse beacon in contrast to the grubby surroundings.

"What shall I do?" he asked Tamar urgently.

"Pretend you're not here," she replied. "Cats can do that, can't they?"

"We are masters of invisibility when it suits us."

"Well, please have it suit you now. Maybe they won't notice you. Heaven knows, if these mortals notice anything, they'd notice how dirty this place is. Look, do you see that one over there? The fat one with that lopsided gold circlet on his head?"

Boabdil squinted. "It doesn't look like gold."

"That's because it hasn't been polished since your grandfather was a kitten. He must be the king."

"He is, and there is our rider, speaking with him. I'm going closer." The cat padded up to the long, low, prettily inlaid table between the two men. On one side the king sat upon a heap of mouse-nibbled cushions; on the other the rider was pacing back and forth angrily, shedding the dust of his journey with every step.

"But surely he must realize that what he asks is impossible!" the king whined. "Go back and tell him so."

The rider—a tall man so sun-browned that his skin now matched his boots—stopped dead in his tracks. "Your Majesty, when I entered your service I told you I was loyal, but

I never told you I was an idiot. He will only order me beheaded and send his armies after you anyway."

"Oh dear, oh dear!" The king wrung his hands. "Why will he not take no for an answer? Does he think I am lying? He is a king, the same as I. One king does not lie to another."

The rider stroked his beard, and a little stream of sand fell to the threadbare carpet. "Perhaps he thinks that you are refusing him the princess's hand in marriage because you want him to pay you more for her. He told me so. He also told me that he is not the kind of man who likes to bargain. Bargaining makes him touchy, and when he feels touchy the only thing that calms him down again is invading someone else's kingdom."

"He didn't happen to mention any one kingdom in particular, did he?" the kind asked, shivering.

The rider let the question pass. "He said that the first price he offered you is more than fair for a wife, especially his twenty-fifth."

"Twenty-fifth or two-hundredth, what is the use? We are doomed. No man was ever so unfortunate as I! Other kings have daughters and daughters and more daughters. I have heard of some so overrun with girl-children that they cannot take a step in their own palace without tripping over six or seven royal princesses. One king is supposed to have gone crazy from all that giggling under one roof. Oh, lucky man! Other kings sigh for sons. Sons!"

He uttered a short, cold laugh. "I have seventy-eight sons, all in good working order. What use are they? Only one can become king after I die, and the rest must go out seeking adventures and slaying giants and rescuing damsels and other such silly heroic stuff. But daughters—! Daughters can become brides. Daughters can marry other kings and make them behave politely to me."

The rider sat down on the low table and pulled off his boots. "This king was not speaking about you politely at all when I left." He turned one boot upside down and spilled out a tiny dune.

"Why should he?" The king propped his fat chin on his fatter hands and looked hopeless. "All I have is one daughter, but ten thousand demons live inside her. All that a daughter can do is get married, but this child of mine says she would sooner die!''

"Uh-oh," thought Boabdil.

"Hush," Tamar instructed him. "There may be more to it than what the king says."

"What more can there be? Only one princess, and she will not marry! Not even when her father's kingdom is in danger of being attacked!''

"Hush, I say. So far we know only what her father has said, and fathers seldom take the time to learn the whole story from their children. I am sure this king told his daughter to marry, she said she would sooner die, and he stalked away, complaining about how mean and cruel and ungrateful children are nowadays. But did he stop feeling sorry for himself long enough to ask her why she refused to marry? I think not. That question is for us."

"Us?" The cat's fur prickled up all down his spine.

"Yes, Boabdil. Now you and I must find our princess."

"But how?" the cat asked. "Grimy and shabby as this palace may be, it's still big! How shall we find—?"

"YOW!"

Tamar's ears were almost split by Boabdil's enraged cry. Her stomach fell, then leaped up in a most upsetting way as she and the cat together were jerked high into the air without a word of warning. The outer world spun dizzily as she saw first the floor dropping away beneath them, then the walls swinging around, and finally the dark, laughing face of the king's rider staring into Boabdil's eyes.

"Well, my fine fellow, and what wind blew you here?" Rough fingers rubbed Boabdil's ears in a friendly manner. Tamar felt the cat go limp as he began to purr.

"Boabdil, keep your eyes open!" she commanded.

"I can't help it," the cat replied. "I always close my eyes when I purr, and I always purr when something feels this nice." The rumbling noise wrapped the genie like a big, warm, woolly blanket.

Through the din of Boabdil's purr, Tamar heard the rider say, "Maybe your royal daughter can be made to see reason."

"Ha!" the king replied. He was beginning to enjoy his

misery. "On the day that wicked child understands I only want what's best for her, cats like that walking mud pie will grow wings."

Boabdil's eyes flew wide for a single, angry instant. "Mud pie!" He stared hard at the king, and Tamar could see the fat little man turn white under the cat's furious scowl. Then the rider resumed scratching Boabdil's ears and the cat fell back into bliss.

"Your Extremely Elevated Highness is not afraid of cats?" the rider asked casually.

"No, no." The king swallowed so loudly that Tamar could hear it even over the sound of Boabdil's pleasure. "I just don't like them, that's all. Horrid, mean, cruel, cunning, unpredictable, selfish, ungrateful things!"

"Is that what you think, my lord?" The rider sounded amused. "True, this is the first cat I have seen in the palace. I always wondered why."

"I have given strict orders to my guards and servants that they are to chase away any of the nasty pests," the king replied, speaking like a man who knows he is always right.

"I see. Which explains . . . you know, Majesty, if you would only bend your rule a bit and allow cats in the royal kitchens, you might be able to hang onto good cooks longer."

"How so?" His Majesty was skeptical.

"There is just something about reaching into the flour bin and scooping out a handful of mice that makes cooks suddenly decide to take their talents elsewhere." When the king merely snorted, the rider went on: "And the princess . . . does she share Your Altitude's opinion of cats?"

The king snorted again. He was very good at it. "I am a firm believer in the theory that children grow up learning from all the living creatures that surround them. Reason enough for me to forbid her to own one of the terrible beasts, even though she has begged for a kitten time after time! She is quite cunning enough as it is, and so selfish—so very selfish that she will not—will not—not even when her own dear father is in danger of being invaded—" He broke down into loud, blubbery sobs full of self-pity.

"Hmmm," said the rider. He stopped petting Boabdil. The cat opened his eyes and uttered a small, annoyed mew. This gave Tamar the chance to observe the thoughtful way the rider was staring at Boabdil. The genie knew a clever mortal when she saw one.

She knew, but that didn't mean she liked it.

8

The princess Nur hugged and kissed and talked baby talk to Boabdil for fifteen minutes straight before she had a sudden second thought. She put the cat down in his basket, sat up tall among her velvet cushions, and narrowed her eyes at the rider.

"What is the catch?" she demanded.

The rider tried to look innocent. "Catch, Your Gracious Highness? I do not know what you mean."

"I think you do know," she said, and gave him a hard look. The rider was tall and strong and hard as leather from his long years of serving Princess Nur's father. Princess Nur was small and pale and a little plump from spending most of her life indoors in her father's palace, whether she liked it or not. Still, she had a way of frowning that made the man turn all cold and shaky inside. It was not easy to look Princess Nur in the eye and lie.

"Flower of Royal Loveliness, if this poor gift should happen to soften your heart just a little and make you more willing to obey your noble father's wishes, would we have to call that a catch?" the rider wheedled.

"Yes, we would." Princess Nur was firm. "My noble father never gives anything to anyone unless he expects to get something better back." She tickled Boabdil's ears lovingly and gazed at the cat with deep yearning, but she said, "I will not marry, and it will take more than a cat to change my mind. Take him away."

"No!" Tamar protested. "She mustn't send us away! Everything will be ruined."

"Don't be afraid," Boabdil advised the genie. "Hear how sadly she said that? She doesn't mean it, and the fellow who brought us here knows it. He's too smart to give up easily."

"But this princess sounds like a mortal who knows what she wants. I do not think he can change her mind."

"Perhaps not. But he understands how to make her change it for herself. Listen!"

They both pricked up Boabdil's ears just in time to hear the rider say, "Very well, Your Highness. I shall take the miserable beast by the scruff of his neck and toss him out of the palace this very instant." He looked at the princess. She did not seem to care. "From a high window," he added. She said and did nothing to contradict him.

He sighed deeply, preparing to use every trick in the book. "What a pity that it is so late in the day. This is the hour when the city streets are the most crowded. If the poor animal is not trampled by a horse or an ox, he might live long enough to be chased to death by the packs of stray dogs that roam the alleys at night. A homeless cat leads a hard life. Still, the clever ones sometimes manage to survive for, oh, a couple of weeks."

The princess's eyes grew wide as she listened to the rider tell of the many dangers waiting for Boabdil in the world outside the palace walls. He saw this, and kept talking. "You should have seen what this creature looked like when your noble father found him, Highness. The poor thing was nothing but bones and fur. 'Take him to the royal kitchens and feed him well!' your noble father said. 'He shall be a special gift for my most beloved daughter.' But if you do not like the cat, I suppose he must go. Come here, you unlucky beggar. You and I have an appointment with a high window." He reached for Boabdil.

Princess Nur gave a loud squawk and threw herself between the king's rider and the cat. "If you dare to touch one whisker of my precious pet's head, your own head will pay for it!" She cuddled Boabdil so close to her chest that the cat squirmed and snarled. "You may tell my father that just because I have accepted his gift does not mean that I will accept his command to marry."

"Certainly not, Your Highness." The rider smiled and bowed as he backed away from the princess. Only when he was at the door of her room did he add, "Sometime I really must tell you about what happens to cats when a war comes." The guards outside the princess's room slammed and bolted the door as soon as the rider was gone.

Princess Nur sat holding Boabdil tightly for longer than the cat could stand it. "I do not believe him," she murmured into the cat's thick fur. "We will not have a war if I do not marry that awful king, and I will not let anything bad happen to you even if we do have a war. Which we will not." Boabdil dug his claws into her arm. It hurt only a little, but it surprised her enough to make her release him. He leaped to the carpet and washed himself vigorously.

"What are you doing, you foolish cat?" Tamar demanded. "You know that she has to stroke you for my plan to work. Get back into her arms this minute!"

"Stroke me, not strangle me." Boabdil kept on licking his pelt. "Don't be so impatient. She will do it soon enough. I know humans. They expect us to ignore them."

The cat was right. Princess Nur fussed over her scratch marks for a few moments, then forgot all about them and started making silly sounds at Boabdil, trying to lure him near. He made her wait, and only when he seemed satisfied with how his fur looked did he walk casually back to her.

Almost at once, she began to stroke him, starting at the head and going all the way to the base of the tail. Boabdil purred, while inside his mind Tamar forced herself to wait until the princess had patted the cat three times. Wishes came in threes, but mortals had somehow gotten the idea that everything else magical had to come in threes as well.

Keeping this in mind, Tamar waited for the third stroke before she used her powers.

It was a pretty spectacular show that Tamar put on for Princess Nur. Three times Boabdil's eyes flashed with green fire. Three times puffs of rainbow smoke burst from his ears. Three times his fur changed color—blue to red to silver—before it went back to its normal shade. Three times Tamar

made the sound of thunderclaps roll from the cat's mouth before she herself sprang out right in front of the gasping princess.

"Hail, O my Master!" Tamar cried, kneeling at the princess's feet. "I am the Slave of the Cat."

"The what?" Nur repeated, coughing a little from all the smoke still lingering in the room. Boabdil stalked away, shaking his ears irritably.

"The Slave of the Cat," Tamar repeated. "I am a genie. Surely you have heard the stories?"

"Heard them? I have read them for myself," the princess replied. She waved her hand, and for the first time Tamar noticed that the walls of Princess Nur's room were lined with well-filled bookshelves. "I adore reading," Nur said. "Sometimes it is the only thing that saves me from dying of boredom. When you are a princess, all they ever expect you to do is wait around to be married, but they never have any good ideas for things to do while you wait."

Tamar laid a finger to her lips thoughtfully and decided to proceed with caution. Mortals who read were usually more crafty than those who did not, and a clever mortal was a dangerous mortal. She made sure that the next thing she said was, "So you know that as my master you cannot use any of your three wishes to wish for more wishes."

"I can't?" The princess looked disappointed.

Mmmm-hmmm, Tamar thought. *Just as I suspected. She's smart enough to have thought of asking for that. Smart, but maybe greedy too. Most mortals are, and that's just what I'm hoping for.* To Nur she only said, "Sorry, those are the rules."

"Oh, dear." The princess's chin sank into her hands. "And there are so many more than three wishes I want to make! I want to be free of this palace, and I want to have a way to take care of myself in the world, and I don't want my father to send his soldiers after me to bring me back, and I really don't want to be a princess anymore, and—oh, pooh, I guess I really ought to wish that my father doesn't have to go to war just because I won't become that other king's twenty-somethingth wife, and I know I don't want to be forced to marry anyone I don't love, and—" She gave

67

Tamar a pleading look. "Could you at least give me some advice on how I could fit all that into three wishes?"

Tamar smiled regretfully. "That would be against regulations. In fact, I should charge you one wish just for asking that. But I won't. I like you. I like you so much that ..."

She paused and looked around the princess's room as if she expected a gang of bandits, armed to the teeth, to spring out from under the floor cushions at any moment. In a spy's most secret whisper she asked, "Can I trust you, O Master? What I am about to offer you is not—not entirely—not at all legal. We magical folk do have our laws. If my fellow genies were to learn of the deal I am about to offer you, it would mean my doom!"

Tamar was very proud of the way she said "doom," making it sound hollow and echoing and chilling, all at the same time. She even threw in a minor roll of thunder to add to the effect of dread she hoped to create. She was sure that the princess would fall to her knees, swear to keep any secret Tamar asked, and beg to know what wonderful bargain the genie had to give.

Instead, Tamar was startled half out of her wits when Nur's response was a calm, "Oh, really? Then perhaps you shouldn't do it at all. Now if you don't mind waiting, I just have to make my three choices."

"Choices?" Tamar echoed, helpless.

"For my wishes," Nur explained. "I cannot have everything I desire with only three wishes, so I must decide which three things I need most."

"But. But. But—but—but—but you can have everything you desire!" the genie exploded.

"No I cannot." Nur folded her hands. "You said so."

"But you can, I say! It would require just one little thing of you, a very small and simple thing—"

"Oh no." The princess wagged a finger at the genie. "You forgot that I have read the tales. You genies are a tricky lot. You would like nothing better than to fool me into squandering the three wishes I do have by promising me more. That will not work. Three wishes will have to be enough for me. I will not be greedy."

"Why not?" Tamar wailed. "You are a mortal! You are

supposed to be greedy! Oh, this is awful. You have made a mess of all my plans. Why can you humans never do what we expect of you? Are you that cruel, or are you only stupid?" She sank down amid the princess's cushions and began to cry.

A jeweled finger tapping Tamar's shoulder roused her from her misery. "I may not know much of the world because I have spent my whole life inside a palace," Nur said, "but I think I know enough to say that you do not sound at all like the Slave of anything, let alone a cat. What are you, really, and what do you want from me?"

Tamar wiped her eyes on the back of her hand, then snapped her fingers. A gold-and-silver silk handkerchief appeared in midair. She blew her nose loudly, then said, "Well, I am indeed a genie."

"So I see," the princess remarked, smiling at the magical handkerchief. "A genie who has gone to a lot of trouble to make me her Master, am I right?"

Tamar nodded, then confessed, "I need your help."

"What help can you need from me?" Nur asked. "You have all the magic of the world at your command; I have twenty different ways to braid hair and paint fingernails. You can circle the world in a thought; I cannot set foot out of these rooms without fifty of my father's best guards to surround me. You have the power to move mountains; I do not have even the power to marry who and when I want, if I want to marry at all. What can I possibly do for you?"

"Well, for one thing," said Boabdil, coming back after having gotten the leftover smoke out of his ears and fur, "you can marry."

9

"**A**re you sure you would not rather change your mind about this, O Master?" Tamar wheedled. It was only the fourteenth time she had posed the question. She did not think Princess Nur had any right to glare at her like that.

"Yes, I am sure!" the princess snapped, and threw a dirty dishrag at the genie. Growling and grumbling, she plunged her hands back into the basin of soapy water and continued to scrub the dishes. From time to time she lifted one hand to push her hair out of her eyes.

Boabdil the cat came strolling into the kitchen as if he owned the entire palace. He thought he did. "Well, ladies, and how are we getting along today?" he asked pleasantly.

Princess Nur flicked a handful of soap bubbles at him and missed. The cat leaped backward, hissing. "It was only a friendly question," he said, then licked invisible foam from his fur.

"Do not pay attention to her." Tamar sounded more than a little bitter as she labored over a stack of plates that needed to be dried. "My wise Master has simply discovered that some wishes are harder to live with than others. Now we are waiting to see how long it takes before she also learns that what one wish bungles, another can make better."

"I thought you said that a new wish can never undo an old," Nur objected.

"That is partly true, O Master." The female genie made an elaborate gesture with her dish towel. "If you wish for a heap of gold and later wish it away, I can do that. In life it is a natural thing for gold to come and go easily. But if you wish for me to destroy your enemies and later on you decide they were not such bad folk after all, I cannot bring them back. Dead is dead and gone is gone. Not all of Solomon's magic can change what is universal law."

Boabdil listened keenly to all of this. "Does that mean that Princess Nur has to be a servant girl forever?"

"Not at all. Servant girls are always turning out to be princesses, in the old tales, so why cannot a princess be a servant girl? Besides, she is not really a servant; she just looks like one." Tamar spoke to the cat as if Princess Nur were a thousand miles away. She knew how easily some mortals became annoyed by people talking about them that way, so she did it on purpose. "My Master has wished—most foolishly, I think—to come into Lord Haroun's house in disguise. Instead of taking the very generous offer I made to her and being content, she had to make things complicated. Most mortals would jump at the chance to have a genie ready to grant their every wish—not just three, but every single wish they might ever desire! Would they ask questions? Would they make conditions?"

"Would they be greedy fools enough to marry a man they have never met just because someone else says it is a good idea?" Nur chimed in. "If I wanted that, I could have stayed in my father's palace and let him pick my husband."

"But if you marry the husband I have chosen for you, you will also get me!" Tamar insisted. "Me and all the wishes you could ever desire. All you would have to do is wish to marry Haroun ben Hasan. What could be simpler?"

"Sorrow is simple," Nur replied. "With happiness, there is always a catch."

Tamar rolled her eyes. "Master, far be it from me to lecture you. A genie is created to hearken and obey. I have stood by silently and watched you waste a perfectly good wish on this—this silly, romantic notion of yours to come into Lord Haroun's palace disguised as a common servant. Why? To see whether I am trying to marry you to some sort of monster? Well, you have seen him. Is he ugly?"

"He is quite handsome," the princess admitted.

"When he wandered through the kitchen and saw you

working, did he speak to you rudely? Or did he behave as if you were just another thing he owns?"

Nur could not lie. "He spoke to me kindly and asked whether I were happy working here. He seems to have a good heart."

"Then what is stopping you from making that one small, easy, insignificant wish—to have him for your husband!—when making it will bring you so much more besides?" Tamar raised her hands to the heavens, tiny starbursts of white light sizzling at her fingertips.

A little smile tickled one corner of the princess's mouth. "Indeed, what is stopping me? I could use one wish to marry Lord Haroun, then use one of the countless wishes you promise me to unmarry him." She gave Tamar a sudden, penetrating stare. "Couldn't I?"

Tamar opened her mouth, closed it, bit her bottom lip, and said nothing.

"I see." Princess Nur went back to scrubbing dishes.

Boabdil rubbed against the genie's ankles. "I think you should tell her the whole story," he said. "She is too smart to settle for less than that."

"Too smart," Tamar echoed bitterly. "Master Ishmael never taught us that princesses could be smart; just beautiful."

"Your Master Ishmael should have spent less time in lamps," Princess Nur remarked. "This world is wide enough for a few smart princesses, too."

Tamar was on the point of leaping to her old teacher's defense when the whole kitchen began to shake and shimmer. Nur gasped, then cried out, "Oh! Oh! Oh! Oh!" in little puffs. Everything was changing. The plain, useful ovens with their black iron doors became bright blue enamel surrounded by pretty tiles shaped and colored like fish scales. All the cookware flashed away, coming back brand-new, pink and green porcelain pots and pans with gold and silver handles. Even the big basins in which Tamar and Nur were washing the dishes changed from plain tin to gorgeously painted ivory.

Then, as suddenly as they had begun, the changes stopped. Princess Nur clutched the edge of her dish basin. "What was that?" She looked down at her clothes—once the simple, dull brown dress of a common servant, now pale green satin robes richer than any she had owned while living in her father's palace—and added: "And what is all this?"

Boabdil peeked out from under the table. "I would guess that our friend Haroun ben Hasan has decided to redecorate his humble home."

The cat had scarcely finished speaking when Haroun himself stuck his head around the edge of the kitchen doorway. "Well, how do you like it?" he asked. For a man who commanded so much wealth and magical power, he sounded remarkably shy and uncertain when speaking to ladies.

Tamar and Nur both bowed low. The genie had been wise enough to disguise herself so that Haroun would not be able to recognize her when she came back into his house. The face she had chosen was not so beautiful as her own— what mortal woman can be as lovely as a creature of magic?—but it was still beautiful. That face was, in fact, copied from a portrait that Tamar had seen hanging in the king's palace. She did not know it was the face of a great queen; she just "borrowed" it because it was the first mortal face she could think of.

This turned out to be a mistake, as she discovered shortly after she looked up and said, "Whatever changes you desire are certainly fine with your humble and obedient servants, O our Master."

Haroun ben Hasan stared at her so intently that he did not seem to hear when Princess Nur said, "We find these changes very attractive, my lord, even if we were not expecting them." Haroun said nothing, still gazing at Tamar.

The princess was irritated. She was not used to being ignored. Motioning to Boabdil, she whispered, "What is the matter with him?"

Seeing Haroun's distracted state, the cat did not even bother to lower his own voice when he replied, "Who can say? As a rule, he does not spend a lot of time in the kitchens. Perhaps he is confused by his surroundings."

"He does not look confused," said Nur.

"Then perhaps he is shy around new faces. You and my lady Tamar are very recent additions to the household staff. New servants are sometimes badly frightened by the effects of his wishes, you know. That is why he came down here in the first place, to see if you were all right."

"That is good of him. But my genie tells me he commands a genie of his own. Why does he need any other servants?"

Boabdil closed his eyes. "Lord Haroun is a kindly man at heart. He can see that granting wishes is sometimes tiring for his genie, and so he decided to hire a few mortal servants to take care of the everyday chores rather than exhaust Khalid—that is his genie's name—by wishing for his bed to be made or his dinner to be cooked or his treasures to be dusted. For these tasks he hires ordinary servants."

Only now, Haroun was obviously discovering that one of his new servants was not quite so ordinary. A great feeling of confusion seized his heart. He felt his head spin. He was sure that he was sweating. His lips were dry, and when he opened his mouth to speak, all he could manage to say was: "Ungkh."

Princess Nur saw how pale he was and became concerned. "Master, are you well?"

"Ungkh," Haroun assured her. He continued to stare at Tamar with a face like a chicken that has run headfirst into a brick wall. Abruptly he recovered himself enough to shout, "Khalid! Khalid! Come to me at once!"

There was a whistling and a rustling as if something very large were flying through the air. The new pots and pans clinked and chinked together, the oven doors rattled on their hinges, and Princess Nur's pile of freshly washed dishes shattered into a million pieces.

Apart from that, nothing happened.

Haroun scowled into the air. "Come here, to me, at once, and make yourself visible," he snarled.

The air between Princess Nur and Haroun ben Hasan shimmered. Khalid stood with hands pressed together and head bowed. "Why did you not say so, O Master?" he asked innocently. "I am here to serve."

"Of course you are," said Haroun in a way that left no doubt about who he thought was the biggest liar the magical world had ever spawned.

"How may I make your life ever more comfortable?"

the genie inquired. "Oh, I know I have just transformed the furnishings of every single room in this miserably tiny palace, exchanged all of the horses in your stable for pure white camels, traded your old brown camels for a fresh crop of horses—all of them identical black stallions with matching red-and-gold saddles and harnesses—and given all of your servants brand new clothes to wear, but think nothing of it! Ask for something else! Ask for anything you like! Do not think for a second that I might get tired, or want a little time to myself. I would only waste it on silly things like resting or thinking or going off to be with my friends. But who needs friends with a Master like you? Go on, wish! Wish for the world!"

"If you want some time to yourself, Khalid, you only have to ask for it," Haroun muttered. He looked embarrassed. "I only wanted to talk to you. Come see me in the Chamber of Ten Thousand Pheasants when you have a moment to spare. I will be waiting." Head pulled into his shoulders like a tortoise, he shuffled off.

"Speak to him 'when you have a moment to spare'?" Tamar wondered aloud. "That does not sound like him at all."

"No, it does not," Khalid agreed, scratching his head. "I suppose I had better go and see what it is he wants. Your pardon, ladies." The genie bowed and vanished.

"Who was that?" Princess Nur asked, grabbing Tamar's sleeve urgently. If the female genie had paid more attention, she might have noticed that the princess was wearing the same stunned-chicken expression as Haroun ben Hasan. But when Khalid was near, Tamar seldom noticed anything but him.

"That was the reason why I have asked you—no, begged you—to be a nice, sensible Master and wish to marry Lord Haroun ben Hasan," Tamar replied. She related the whole sad tale of Khalid's captivity, ending by telling the princess about just what it would take to guarantee Haroun's perfect happiness.

"*Me?*" Princess Nur shrilled.

"Do you see any other spare princesses around?" Boabdil asked.

"No, oh no!" Nur protested. "It is impossible, unthinkable!"

"But why?" Tamar implored, clasping the princess's hands. "You have seen Lord Haroun, you have agreed he is neither ugly nor unkind. Wish to marry him, and I know he will be a good husband. He will certainly be a grateful one. His heart's desire is to marry a royal lady. You mortals do not value the wishes you get from genies. You think you have magical gifts coming to you! Yet when one mortal grants the dearest wish another mortal yearns for—oh, the thanks! The lifetime of gratitude! To say nothing"—Tamar lowered her voice and looked sly—"of the lifetime of wishes I shall grant you. For all of this, why can you not wed Lord Haroun and free my poor Khalid?"

Princess Nur looked at the floor. "Because I love another."

Tamar's mouth fell open in shock. Her lips trembled with unasked questions; unasked because she was afraid she already knew the answer. Then she let out a shriek loud enough to split the heart of the desert and ran out of the kitchens.

The cat Boabdil looked up casually from washing his front paws. He cocked is head at Nur. "Let me guess: You love Khalid."

"My heart leads, and I must follow," the princess answered, spreading her hands helplessly.

"Of course." Boabdil bit off the words as short as if they were a tender mouse tail. "You know you won't be able to wish Khalid free," he told her.

"No?"

"No. One genie's magic can not undo the work of another's. Not unless they have a full-scale battle, and that is something far too noisy and messy to happen often." He gave his left paw another lick. "I hate messes."

"Can I wish for Lord Haroun to free him, then? Or wish that Khalid become a mortal man? Or that I become a genie? I just know I would not mind being a prisoner forever if I could be with him." She made cow-eyes at the doorway through which Khalid had departed.

"No," the cat said. "Those wishes (lick) go against (lick, lick) the natural order of things."

"And I suppose a talking cat is natural?" the princess sneered.

"Well, people (lick) have often thought we *could* talk (lick) or *should* talk (lick) or *can* talk but are too clever to let mere humans in on the secret. We are certainly (lick, lick) smarter than some creatures who do chatter. Besides (lick), if it went against the natural order of things (lick, lick, gnaw claws) for me to speak, I would not (lick) be speaking now. The magic would have simply (lick) gone to waste."

"Falling in love is natural," said Nur in a terribly moony, drippy voice. "Perhaps I shall wish for Khalid to fall in love with me."

"Wonderful." Boabdil's word was dry as a sandstorm. "Then he will not be just a captive, but a lovesick captive, too. I cannot tell you how very, very much better that will make him feel!" He finished with his left paw and added: "Anyway, it wouldn't work."

"Love is natural!" the princess objected.

"But forced love is not," the cat countered. "If it were, you could force yourself to love Lord Haroun as easily as you claim you love Khalid. It would be the better bargain. By the bye"—Boabdil looked honestly interested—"why do you love Khalid? It is rather sudden, I think."

"Why do I love—?" Nur seemed unable to believe the question. "Why, because he is—he is so handsome—"

"So is Lord Haroun."

"—and so kind—"

"How would you know? You have seen more of Lord Haroun's kindness."

"—and so well-spoken—"

"Yes, I think he must have said three whole sentences to you."

—"and so—so"—she clasped her hands "so sad, so hopeless, so beautifully, beautifully tragic!"

Boabdil made a face. "Well, at least now I see what sort of books they allow princesses to read. Soppy stuff and romantic nonsense. It is a miracle that you did not decide to marry the first beggar you found in the street outside your father's palace. You would have assumed he was a prince in disguise!" He stalked away, tail high, muttering to himself about princesses.

Alone in the kitchens, Princess Nur found a chair and sat down with a sigh. "I *do* love Khalid," she told the air. "And I *do* have a good reason for loving him. I know I just saw him now, but has no one in this place ever heard of love at first sight? And I know I do not love Lord Haroun. For one thing he is—he is—" She searched her mind for something about Haroun ben Hasan that made him impossible to love. She had no luck. "Well, there must be *something* wrong with him, or my genie would not be trying to force me to marry him. Oh, she is just like my father! 'You must marry this king! You must marry that prince! You have to marry the man I choose. You cannot choose a husband for yourself.' I am very tired of having all of my choices made for me. For once, I have made the choice, and I choose to love Khalid!" She folded her arms across her chest, very pleased with herself.

And a very good choice it is, said the air.

Princess Nur jumped up. "Who is it? Who is there?"

A friend. The voice came from everywhere and nowhere. It echoed inside the ovens and tinkled amid the pieces of broken china on the floor. *A friend who only desires your perfect happiness.*

If Princess Nur was afraid, she did not let it show. She knew that Lord Haroun's palace was a place of magic. Unseen voices were to be expected. Bravely she said, "If you are my friend, show yourself! Only enemies skulk in shadow."

A sigh like a small sandstorm gusted through her hair. *So suspicious. Very well, my lady. If that is what you wish . . . Hearkening and obedience.*

There was a rumble like thunder; the floor shook beneath Nur's feet until she had to grab the edge of a table to stay upright. Invisible demons howled in her ears, and from the corner of her eye she thought she saw flaming skeletons dance all around the room. A lesser girl would have fallen to her knees, hidden her face, and sobbed. Princess Nur was not that courageous, but she was stubborn. Clearly the unseen being that was causing all these frightening sights and sounds wanted her to be badly scared. She refused to give it the satisfaction of seeing her shiver, shudder, or shake.

"Well?" she shouted over the howling demons—shouted so loudly, in fact, that the dancing skeletons paused in mid-prance to stare at her with smoking, empty eyesockets. "What is taking you so long to appear? If you cannot handle so simple a spell as making yourself visible, I do not think you have the power to give me the happiness you promise, 'friend.' "

The howling and the rumbling stopped, the fiery skeletons crumbled to ashes, the thunder died away. Princess Nur found herself gazing up at the biggest, ugliest, nastiest-looking creature she had ever seen.

"Who—*what* are you?" she asked.

"You may call me Gamal," the thing said. "I am a genie. Could you not tell?" In one clawed hand he held a brass lamp, but with the other he indicated his jeweled turban and rich, gauzy garments.

"You, a genie? But you do not look—" Princess Nur stopped herself. The only other genies she had met were Tamar and Khalid. She had no idea that such beautiful beings could have so repulsive a relative as this Gamal. It was not his face and body alone that made him so hideous, but the way every word he spoke sounded like a cruel taunt. His expression, too, made the princess recall one of the palace servants who was always spreading mean gossip and who only smiled when someone else got hurt. "That is, I mean, you are so much more impressive than any genie I ever saw," she managed to add. Ugly and awful he might be, but he was also magical. Magic could mean danger.

Her words seemed to please him. "So I am. You are wise, for a princess. It will be my pleasure to serve you."

"Oh, I do not think that will be necessary," Nur said quickly. She had no specific reason, but she just knew that the less she had to do with Gamal, the better off she would be. "That would be greedy of me. I already have a genie."

"I know." Gamal sounded bored.

"You do?"

"Of course. Your genie is a dear, close, personal friend

of mine. Oh, she is nowhere near as powerful as I am, but that is why I like to look out for her."

You mean spy on her, Nur thought. She decided to walk very carefully until she could get rid of Gamal.

"I am also a dear, dear friend of Khalid's," Gamal went on. "We three were in school together. Ah, happy schooldays! It breaks my heart to see what has happened to poor Khalid. I do not think he should have to suffer so long for one small mistake, do you?"

The moment Gamal mentioned Khalid's name, Princess Nur forgot all about mistrusting him. She thought that he sounded sincere when he spoke of how sorry he was for his old schoolmate's plight. A few fat tears trickled down the ugly genie's face and vanished. Nur's common sense vanished with them.

"Oh yes, I do think it is awful!" she cried. "If you are his friend, can you not do something to free him?"

"Alas," was all that Gamal said, and two more tears slithered from his eyes.

"Hmph! Then a fat lot of good your promises are." Nur folded her arms and stuck out her lower lip. "You offer me perfect happiness, yet you say you cannot free Khalid!"

"Does your happiness really depend on whether he is free or not?" Gamal spoke persuasively. "You would be happy to be a prisoner yourself if only you would be with him; you said so. That is what you want: To be with Khalid forever. Am I wrong, my lady?"

Somehow, hearing her words repeated by Gamal, Princess Nur no longer thought the idea sounded quite so good. "It would be nicer if we were both free," she said.

"Oh, so it would! But how can that be, dear lady?" Gamal's smile was extremely oily. "Khalid will not be free until his Master is happy. His Master will not be happy until he has married a princess. You are the only princess around, and if you marry Lord Haroun, you cannot have Khalid too. Such a sticky, sticky problem." He held up one claw. "How lucky you are that sticky problems are my specialty. I do so want to help you."

Princess Nur decided that, monster or no monster, she was going to get a straight answer out of Gamal, and so she asked him point-blank: "Khalid is your old friend, not I; why help me at all? Why not just help him?"

"Clever girl," Gamal purred. "Too clever," he growled under his breath. In a warmer tone he said, "Khalid is much too proud to accept my help. You see, he was not—not exactly one of the best students in our class. Now I, on the other hand, was—"

"I am sure you were," said Nur, eager to cut short Gamal's boasting. "Very well, I believe you. I must, for you are my only hope. What must we do?"

"We can do nothing until you do something first."

"What?"

"What mortals do best: Make a wish."

The princess was skeptical. Gamal had won her over with the tears he had shed for his "dear friend" Khalid, but a small voice in the back of Nur's head had begun to whisper, Cannot a creature who is able to make gold appear out of thin air make tears appear as well? "And if I make it, you will grant it?" she demanded.

Gamal smiled at her as if she were a child. "Fair one, how could I? You yourself admit that you already have a genie serving you. She must grant the wish you make. Those are the rules. The Council whose word governs all genies and other magical beings would have my head if I gave you any wishes at all."

"I was given three," said Nur. "I used the first to have my genie take me from my father's palace in such a way that no one would notice I was gone or worry about me. I used the second to have her disguise us both so that we could enter Lord Haroun's palace as servants because—well, the reason does not concern you. I have only one wish remaining. Why should I squander it on your say-so?"

"But that is the beautiful thing!" Gamal laughed. "It will not be squandered, for I shall tell you *exactly* how to word it so that it brings you everything you desire. Who knows how to get the most out of wishes better than a genie? Yes, wish for just what I tell you and I swear by all King Solomon's power that you will have your perfect happiness."

Nur raised one eyebrow. "That is a big promise."

"I am a big genie," Gamal replied. "And I am your friend. I risk much by making you this offer. We are not supposed to help humans make their wishes; those are the rules. If the Council found out, I would be in trouble. Oh, they are most terribly strict, the Council, and the punishments they give are horrible!" He turned the lower portion of his body into smoke so that he could come down to Nur's eye level and say, "The risk is mine, the gain all yours—and Khalid's! Will you do it?"

"I do not know." Princess Nur did not like having Gamal's eyes so close to hers. It was like peering into two huge yellow bonfires. "I need time to think."

Gamal's lips twitched impatiently, but immediately he turned his scowl into a smile. "Take all the time you like," he said. "Behold! I shall even give you a little gift just to show you that you can trust me." He reached into the folds of his robe and brought out a plain ring. It was not gold or silver, but dull iron. Nur did not think it was much of a gift from a creature who could make all the riches of the world appear as easily as blinking.

Gamal seemed to read her thoughts. "No, it is not much to look at," he said. "But I promise you, that ring contains great power. It was dipped in the Fountain of Eternal Love."

"I have heard of the Fountain of Eternal Youth," Nur admitted, studying the ring. "Never the Fountain of Eternal Love." She gave Gamal a hard stare. "If I put this on, it will not make me fall in love with whoever gives it to me, will it?"

"Perish the thought!" Gamal's smile grew a little tighter. "No one can force love, even by magic. But if you are able to make someone say that he loves you, then give him this ring to wear, his love will never fade; it will be eternal, like the stars that dance in the heavens." He laid the ring on his palm and held it out to her. "Will you do me the honor of accepting this gift and thinking about the other offer I have made?"

Nur hesitated, then took the ring from Gamal's palm as if it were red hot. It looked huge, yet when she slipped it on her finger it shrank to fit perfectly. A strange golden glow appeared to pulse from the ring for a few moments, and for an instant Nur thought she heard a plaintive voice crying in her ear, *Free! Set me free!*, but then both the voice and the glow vanished. She dared to look Gamal in the eye and said, "Thank you." She did not sound at all sure about it.

Gamal acted as if she had given him an hour's worth of the most sincere thanks in the world. Bowing until his great forehead nearly touched the floor, he begged her to take all the time she wanted to think over his offer of help. "When you have made up your mind and want to call me back, you have only to summon me by name. Farewell, dear lady, and may you have everything your heart ever wishes." So saying, he was gone.

Princess Nur stood where she was for a time, thinking about what had just happened. She could not take her eyes off the iron ring. There was something about it that made her skin itch; her brain itched too.

"Maybe I ought to speak to my genie about this Gamal and his gift," she said, thinking out loud. "Genies are famous for playing tricks on humans, and I still do not trust him." She pondered awhile, then added, "No. No, I think I will keep this as my own secret. If Gamal is telling the truth, this ring is more valuable than gold. And how do I know that I can trust my genie any more than I can trust Gamal? She, too, loves Khalid. If I ask her about this ring, she might lie, and tell me it is worthless, just to take it for herself to use on him!" Nur sighed. "That is the problem with genies: Sometimes they are as bad as people."

We are not! the ring chirped indignantly, but Princess Nur had gone back to washing dishes and did not hear. She plunged her hands into the water and could not notice when a tiny trail of bubbles gurgled up out of the iron ring to mingle with the soapy foam already in the basin.

10

In the Chamber of Ten Thousand Pheasants, Khalid listened to what his Master had to say and tried to keep a straight face. Laughing at his Master would be very rude and not the sort of behavior expected of a professional genie. Besides, Lord Haroun was being extremely kind to him all of a sudden, even to the point of telling the genie to lie back on one of the green damask-covered couches and help himself to a cup of sherbet. If Khalid laughed at his Master now, it would probably mean back to work, several dozen new wishes to fulfill, and no more sherbet.

It was very good sherbet—lime and pecan, Khalid's favorite flavor. The genie served himself a second helping and asked, "So, when did you decide that your new servant is really a princess in disguise?"

"I did not *decide* anything," Haroun replied. "She is what she is!"

There was no arguing with that. Khalid licked his ivory spoon and tapped it on the edge of the frosty silver cup. "What I meant, O Master, is how can you tell she is a princess? Even in the best houses of this city, no one has a princess washing the dirty dishes."

Haroun rolled his eyes as if asking the sky to witness what a thickheaded genie he was saddled with. "Well, of course no *normal* princess lives in someone else's palace and washes dirty dishes!"

"I see," said Khalid. "We have an *abnormal* princess."

Haroun made a sound like a tiger who has just backed

into a bramble bush. "What we have is an *enchanted* princess! I would think that you of all beings would recognize magic when it shares the same roof. Oh, this is the opportunity of a lifetime! Princesses are *always* going and getting themselves enchanted. You know how it is: if you turn your back on them for an instant, half of them are frogs and the other half are washing dishes."

"What good luck that we do not have one of the froggier kind, then." Khalid leaned forward, holding out his dish. "May I please have some more sherbet?"

Haroun was so absorbed by his great good fortune that he served Khalid with his own hands."This is wonderful, wonderful!" he exclaimed excitedly. "Some evil magician has placed the lady under a spell. Perhaps it is the Grand Vizier himself who is responsible. It is usually the Grand Vizier in these cases. He wanted to marry her, but she refused him because she did not love him, so he had an evil magician turn her into a common household servant. The spell is powerful, but it can be broken by—by—" Haroun searched the air for an answer and could not find one. He turned to Khalid. "How *can* this spell be broken?"

"How should I know?" the genie replied, his mouth full of lime-pecan sherbet.

A glob of sherbet, catapulted from Lord Haroun's spoon, caught Khalid right between the eyes. "What do you mean, 'How should I know?' you miserable, worthless puff of smoke?" Haroun jumped up from his couch, face red with rage. "You are a *genie!* Genies are supposed to know all about spells and enchantments."

"I can tell you this much," Khalid said, wiping the sherbet out of his eyes. "You can never break a spell by throwing a tantrum. A window, yes; a spell, no."

"Oh." Haroun's shoulders sagged. "I apologize. But oh, my friend, if you only knew how upset I am!" He folded his hands over his heart. "The moment I saw her face, I knew her for what she was and I adored her on the spot. That face, so full of royal beauty! None but a true princess could have a face like that."

Khalid thought of all the pictures of princesses that Master Ishmael had shown the class when they were studying

King Solomon and His Friends 101: The Special Require-ments of Royal Wishes. Some of the regal ladies had been fat, some thin, some dark, some fair, some lovely as the dawn, some difficult to tell apart from their pet monkeys. (In his heart, Khalid still blamed the odder-looking prin-cesses for how he had mistaken the cat Boabdil for a human being; for one thing, the cat had been prettier than some of them, more graceful than most, less hairy than others.) If there was such a thing as one specific type of face that said "Pay No Attention to the Dirty Dishes; I Am Really a Prin-cess," Khalid had missed it.

Still, if his master wanted to believe that one of the new servants was an enchanted princess, he was not going to say a word.

On second thought, he *would* say a word; several. Here was a chance too good to let escape. "O my Master," he said, floating up from his couch and gliding over to the lovestruck mortal. "Your words overjoy my heart. Not every man is wise enough to recognize a true princess when she has been so well disguised by the spells of an evil Grand Vizier."

"An evil magician," Haroun corrected. "The evil magi-cian's spells are *bought* by the evil Grand Vizier."

"Just so. As I was saying, I have known for a long time that your wisdom is greater than that of King Solomon him-self. If anyone can break the spell, it is you. That is why I have brought this unlucky princess into your home."

"You, Khalid? You are the one who brought her here?" Haroun's eyes were wide. "But I thought old Yazid was in charge of hiring new workers."

Khalid put on a mysterious smile. "To please a good, dear, generous Master, I thought that this once I could do a better job of hiring than old Yazid. It was . . . a little surprise for you."

"Oh, best of genies, I see your plan now! How clever you are! You have brought the enchanted princess here so that I can break the spell on her and she will fall in love with me for myself alone. My heart's desire will be fulfilled!"

"Mine also," Khalid murmured. Aloud he said, "And when you have your heart's desire, O Master, then do I dare to hope that you will remember your promise to me?"

"Never doubt it!" Haroun cried. "As soon as my princess admits she loves me, I will grant you your freedom. What is more, here and now I *wish* that as soon as the princess says, 'I love you, Lord Haroun,' my very next words will be, 'I wish that Khalid be set free.' Can you ask for more?"

"Indeed not," said the genie. "Hearkening and obedience." The air between them shimmered momentarily as Haroun's wish was officially inscribed in the invisible books where such things are recorded.

Haroun rubbed his hands together. "Now I shall go to her and speak of love. Oh, not at once—such things must be done step by step. We shall start by discussing the weather."

"An excellent idea, O my Master," said Khalid. "We have been having so much weather lately."

Lost in his dream of romance, Haroun went on without hearing the genie's words. "It shall be just as it happens in the tales—no, better! I shall not let her know that I know her true identity; not right away. Nor do I want her to love me just because I will be the one to break her spell. By the way, Khalid, I do not suppose I could simply wish for the spell to be broken?"

Khalid shook his head. "We genies cannot use our wishes against one another or against the spells of mortal magicians. That would be cheating. However, I believe there are only so many different ways of breaking such spells, according to the stories."

"Yes, yes; a kiss is the usual method. I think I can handle that."

"But . . . suppose it is not?" Khalid suggested. "I have heard some tales in which a kiss only serves to make the spell that much tighter. Why, there was even one story in which an ill-timed kiss made the enchanted princess fall in love with the *next* man she met, leaving the first suitor to die horribly, of a broken heart."

"Horribly?" Haroun's chin quivered.

"Oh, most horribly; no doubt about that. They say his bleached bones still lie in the desert."

Trying to sound as if he treated the whole tale lightly, Haroun said, "There are no stories where the man finds the princess in the middle of the desert!"

Khalid smirked. "I know that. He went into the desert afterward, to forget his broken heart. His camel ate him."

"Camels do *not* eat—"

"It was a special case, and a very excitable camel." The genie sounded so sure of himself that Haroun had to believe he was speaking the truth. "With respect, O my Master, I have been alive so much longer than you that I might have changed your great-great-great-great-great-grandfather's diapers. Not that I would have wanted to. I have forgotten more stories than you will ever hear, each and every one of them about enchanted princesses and how to break the spells that hold them. It was wrong of me, before, to pretend ignorance. I only wanted to finish my sherbet in peace. The truth of things is, when it comes to enchanted princesses, I have all the answers."

"You do?" Haroun's voice rose hopefully. "Then—then you must know how to break the spell on this one! Tell me at once! I order, I command, I *wish* you would!"

"Hearkening and obedience, Master," said Khalid; and he floated back to his couch and said nothing else for a long, long time.

"Well?" Haroun demanded after the genie had finished off two additional dishes of sherbet. "I await!"

"So you do," said Khalid, not at all concerned. "I have heard your wish. I am fulfilling it even as we speak."

"What you are doing," said Haroun testily, "is sitting on *my* couch in *my* palace eating all of *my* lime-pecan sherbet. You are supposed to be telling me how to break the spell on my beloved princess."

"Yes," said Khalid. "So I shall. As soon as I remember it." He nibbled the tip of his ivory spoon, gazed at the painted ceiling of the Chamber of Ten Thousand Pheasants, and hummed an irritating little tune.

Lord Haroun began to curse.

"Oh my Master, why use such language? You are only making my task harder." Khalid set down his sherbet dish and spoon. "I have the answer you seek, but memory is like a merchant's caravan: every treasure, from greatest to smallest, is tucked away in its proper place. There it waits for the merchant to recall precisely where he packed it—is it in this

89

saddlebag or in that chest? Is it locked in that steel strongbox or wrapped in a handkerchief and stuffed in his pocket? He can find it, but not right away; not if *some* people are standing over him, yelling for him to hurry up all the time."

"Wise merchants make a note of where things are packed," said Haroun, a nasty, sharp edge to his voice.

To Haroun's surprise, Khalid rose like a whirlwind from his couch and swept his Master up in a joyful embrace. "Ah! The powers witness that I spoke the truth when I called my Master wiser than King Solomon himself," the genie exclaimed. "A note! Yes, of course, that is it! Oh, the princess is as good as restored already! Invite the wedding guests, call the musicians, order the bridal feast, for you shall have your royal bride before you know it!" Still carrying Haroun, Khalid summoned up a cloud of blue-green smoke that engulfed them both.

"Where are we?" Haroun asked, coughing, when the smoke cleared and Khalid finally set him down.

"Need you ask, O my Master?" The genie gestured at the walls of the room in which they now stood. From floor to ceiling there were nothing but well-packed bookshelves, and the floor itself was a maze of towering bookcases. By the windows stood a table, a reading lamp, and a single comfortable chair. Khalid promptly selected a book from one of the shelves and plopped himself down.

"What are you doing?" Haroun stood before his genie with arms crossed and foot tapping.

Khalid looked up from the book in his lap and smiled mildly. "I am obeying your wish, O my Master. I am seeking the way to break your princess's spell. This library contains all the tales of enchanted princesses that ever were told. These books, like the packing notes the wise merchant makes, shall jog my memory. It will not take me too long— I read quickly—*provided that I am not disturbed!* Now, may I get back to my work?"

"Oh." Haroun looked guilty. "Certainly, certainly. Do not let me interfere, O most excellent of servants. I apologize for having bothered you with foolish questions." He started to back out of the library. "Uh—you did say this would not take very long?"

"Not if I am left in peace," Khalid replied. "Do not worry, O my Master; I shall call you at once when I have found the answer. Or if I need anything." He wiggled his fingers, and a small silvery bell shaped like a lily flower appeared on the table. "I will ring for you. In the meanwhile, did you not say something about going to talk with your princess?"

"Oh, yes. I almost forgot. How silly of me. Yes, I was just going to talk to her about—about—"

"The weather," the genie reminded him.

"Yes, yes, yes, that is right, the weather." Haroun nearly tripped over his own feet as he left the room. The last Khalid heard of him, his Master was practicing saying things like, "It is never the heat, but the humidity; do you not agree?" and "Personally I do not think the rain will hurt the rhubarb."

Very pleased with himself, Khalid settled back in his chair with a good book. "This is perfect," he said to himself. "At last I can have some time off. A week will do, or two. Then I shall find out more about the servant girl with whom my Master seems to have fallen in love. At least he is no longer in love with Tamar."

At the thought of her, he turned from his book and gazed out the window. There was a pretty little garden, one of many within the palace walls. Flowering persimmon trees perfumed the air. White gazelles wandered between rows of gardenia bushes and ate most of the blossoms. Parrots perched amid the fronds of tall palms and had screaming contests to see who could make the gazelles jump the highest. It was all very beautiful and impressive, but Khalid saw none of it.

A vision of Tamar's face hovered over the little garden, her beauty making everything else dull by comparison. Her smile went straight to his heart. It hurt so badly that he had to look away and force himself to think of other things.

"*Could* this servant girl be an enchanted princess?" he wondered. A triumphant smile lit his face. "Ha! That does not matter. If she *is* a princess, a kiss will break the spell— it always does, in spite of what I told my Master—and he can marry her. He is not so bad for a mortal, so why would she not marry him? Then I will be free. And if she is *not* a princess"—Khalid's smile grew brighter—"if she is not a princess, that does not matter either, for I shall use my magic to turn her *into* a princess! I know she will not object—what servant would be unhappy to trade a tub of dirty dishes for a lifetime of luxury?—and my Master will be none the wiser. Not even the Council will be able to find any rule of magic against this! He wished for a princess, a princess he shall have! And I—I shall have my freedom."

Chuckling merrily, Khalid began to page through his book. He was looking forward to his well-earned two-weeks' vacation.

11

"**T**wo weeks," Khalid groaned as he hung by his heels from the kitchen ceiling. "Two miserable weeks straight from the lowest pit of eternal torment! Ay, me, not even the Council themselves could come up with a punishment as devilish as these past two weeks have been!"

The cat Boabdil, who was racing through the kitchens in hot pursuit of a plump mouse, heard the voice from on high and stopped in his tracks. Looking up, he saw only the bunches of fresh herbs that were drying from the rafters. He twitched his whiskers, first in puzzlement, then as he let his most excellent nose sift through the various layers of scent until he discovered . . .

"Oh, it's you, Khalid," he said, addressing a fat bunch of dusty green thyme. "What are you doing up there dressed like a salad?"

"Hiding," the thyme replied.

"Mmmmm." Boabdil did not have to ask the obvious question. He knew from whom Khalid was hiding. The whole household knew, including old Yazid, and he never noticed anything except a late dinner. "She is still after you, is she?"

"Day and night." The thyme shuddered, losing a handful of leaves. Then Khalid gave up on his disguise and returned himself to his original shape. Still upside-down, he told the cat of his misery.

"I was so hopeful, at first! By using my wits alone I have bought myself a little time free of my Master's constant wishes. How was I to know that *she* would hear of it? One day of freedom I had—two at the most!—before she learned that I was working in the library. Two scant days of pleasure, being able to come and go as I liked, given all the books I cared to read—I was always very fond of books, Boabdil—allowed to help myself to anything I desired to eat or drink. My Master was so eager for me to get on with my task that he said I could have a servant of my very own to take care of my wishes! *My* wishes!"

"And of course, knowing what you know of wishes, you told your Master to let the servant have a little freedom, too?" Boabdil purred maliciously.

Khalid scowled at him, but upside-down it looked like a twisted smile. "This servant did not want any freedom, once she knew whom she must serve. The moment she set eyes on me, she began to—to—" The memory made his face go pasty.

"—recite poetry," Boabdil finished the sentence for him. "We know. We all heard her."

"*Love* poetry!" Khalid made a little gagging sound. "Romantic verses written by the masters of the art, no less. She also sang songs of love. Did you know that she can play the lute all by herself?"

"I have never heard of anyone playing the lute in teams," the cat murmured.

Khalid did not hear the barb. "Where does a common servant pick up such things?"

The cat's whiskers curved up into an unnatural grin. "A *common* servant does not. What does that lead you to believe, my friend? Think, now."

Khalid thought. All the possibilities streamed through his brain until— "Oh, no. No!" He did a somersault down from the ceiling and landed on his knees before the cat. "Tell me it is not so, Boabdil! Tell me that she is not—that she cannot be—that it is her companion who is truly—"

"The enchanted princess?" Boabdil preened himself with one paw. "No. Neither one of them is that."

Khalid toppled forward like a felled tree. The cat had to leap nimbly out of the way to avoid being crushed. As he circled the sobbing genie, Boabdil added, "If it is any consolation, she *is* a princess. Not exactly enchanted—I suppose it does not count if she had the spell put on herself, without the benefit of a wicked magician and an evil Grand Vizier—but she is still a princess for all that."

"She?" Khalid lifted his head from the floor. "You mean, the one who has been after me is the princess?"

"She is."

"And the other—the one my master has been courting for these past two weeks is—?"

"Not a princess. She is actually—"

Khalid did not wait to hear the rest. "Oh, what does it matter who or what that one is? She can still serve my purposes. I will go to her at once, Boabdil, and make her a very generous offer: Wed my Master, say nothing of her true identity, and once he has freed me, I shall transform her into as good a princess as ever was, enchanted or not. Ha!" He sat up and folded his arms in triumph. "I should have thought of this sooner. What could be simpler?"

Cats cannot snicker, but Boabdil managed to come close. "I could not recommend that course of action, my friend. You would not like the results."

"And why not?" This time Khalid's scowl worked properly. "Who are you to tell me how to use my magic? You are only a cat!"

"Only a cat," Boabdil slowly repeated the phrase in a way that made it sound more magnificent and awe-inspiring than the hundred empty titles of a king. "But a cat who has known enough genies to also know that outside of a battle of magics, one genie's spells cannot change the effects of another's."

"Another genie's spells?" Khalid was definitely at sea. "The servant girl my Master loves is *not* a princess but *is* enchanted? What genie would want to enchant a servant girl?"

"Does the name Tamar ring any bells?" Boabdil was enjoying himself. It was the nature of cats to play with their prey, teasing the mice they caught with the illusion of possible escape. Some of the mice did get away, but the best part of the game was the playing, not the winning. Now Boabdil had discovered that the game of cat-and-mouse played just as well when it was cat-and-genie.

"Tamar!" The shocked look on Khalid's face was very satisfying. "*She* has enchanted the girl?"

Boabdil decided that it was time to let his prey go. "She *is* the girl, O my friend."

The sound of Khalid's cry was loud enough to bring old Yazid into the kitchen to ask whether dinner was ready yet. All he found there was his master's cat sitting beside a very crumpled bunch of thyme. The old man left, grumbling.

Once old Yazid had gone, Khalid returned to his proper shape. "Tamar! Oh, how can it be she? It was bad enough when my Master fell in love with her while she was herself, but to have him love her in disguise as well—!" The genie looked like a shipwrecked sailor whom the waves have battered badly. "Why has she come back?"

"That should be obvious." Boabdil put on a superior air, superior even for a cat. "She is trying to free you by bringing your master the one thing he desires: a princess." The cat's whiskers drooped a bit as he added, "Alas, her plan does not seem to have worked out in quite the way she had hoped."

A tear rolled down Khalid's cheek. "Now I shall never be free."

Boabdil leaped into the genie's lap, then onto his shoulder. He purred as loudly as he could, to give comfort, and dabbed the tear away with one velvet paw. "Do not despair, my friend. Hope must never die."

"Why should I hope?" Khalid asked in a hollow voice. "What have I to hope for?"

Boabdil snorted. "More than most poor mortals! If you would only stop feeling sorry for yourself, you might be able to see that. Fool, you are loved! How many beings—mortal or magical—are lucky enough to say the same? Tamar loves you, and may my nose lose its cunning if you do not love her, too." The cat tilted his head to one side. "You *do* love her, do you not?"

"With all my heart," the genie sighed.

"Well, then!" Boabdil was pleased. "Two hearts with one desire, two creatures of great magic with one goal—what can stop you? Unless it be your own foolishness. Go to her, my friend. Tell her what is in your heart. Save your pride for another day. After all she has done for you, you owe her that much honesty."

For the first time in nearly two weeks, Khalid looked truly cheerful. "Boabdil, you are right. I shall do as you say, tell Tamar of my love, and see if together we cannot at last break the chain of wishes that binds me to Lord Haroun's service. Ah, to think I—greatest student in Master Ishmael's class—should have to learn wisdom from a cat!"

"Where better?" Boabdil purred. He butted Khalid's cheek. Just then, Princess Nur peeped around the side of one of the big kitchen doors. She was carrying a lute and she stared at Khalid with a terrible yearning in her eyes.

"Uh-oh," said the genie.

Boabdil butted him again. "Do not dare to vanish. Tamar is not the only one to whom you owe honesty. To live without hope is cruel, but it is crueler to allow anyone to live with false hope."

Khalid's eyes met Nur's; he swallowed hard. Setting the cat down on the floor, he stood up and approached the girl. She was quick to bow and ask if she could fetch him anything. He shook his head.

"Then perhaps you would not object if I were to entertain you?" she offered, showing him the lute. "A simple song, to pass the time?" Her fingers brushed the strings in the opening notes of yet another love song.

Khalid laid his hand over the lute strings, making them silent. "I have something to tell you," he said.

Lord Haroun was wandering aimlessly through the palace, trying to think of a rhyme for his latest love poem when he heard the sound of sobbing. It was coming from the smallest of the gardens where herbs and vegetables grew for use in the palace kitchens. Here no gazelles or peacocks walked, no fountains played, no rare and exotic flowers bloomed. There were no benches, and very little shade.

Benches or no benches, someone was sitting in the kitchen garden and crying. Haroun recognized the new servant girl at once. She was seated on the lip of the well that stood in the center of the garden, a lute at her feet. For a moment he hesitated—some people did not like company when they wept—but then his generous heart encouraged him to go into the garden and see what was wrong. *Perhaps it will get my mind off my own troubles,* he reasoned.

He did his best to act as if coming into the garden were his own idea. Humming a bright tune, he made a great business of examining every other bush, shrub, or row of radishes he passed. He pinched leaves, plucked stems, and uprooted nearly half the lettuces before turning to the weeping girl and exclaiming, "Oh! Excuse me. I did not see you sitting there."

"Did you not?" Nur sniffled. "Then either you are blind, or you think I am stupid." She kicked the lute.

"I *beg* your pardon!" Haroun felt as if she had kicked him in the chest instead.

"Beg away." She gave the lute another kick. It rolled over in the dust, strings jangling. "You might make a better beggar than you do an actor. I am the biggest thing in this garden, and you did not see me? Take that tale to another marketplace!" She looked away from him and twisted the strange dark ring on her finger.

Haroun sat down beside her. "I was only trying to see if there was anything I could do to help you. You sounded so miserable." He took a deep breath and let it out slowly. "Is there?"

Nur kept twisting the ring. "What help do I need? I am rich. I have great men—kings!—begging to marry me. I have the powers of magical beings at my command."

"Have you been sitting out in this strong sun long?" Haroun inquired.

Nur's eyes snapped as she jerked her gaze up to meet his. "I am *not* crazy!"

"No, certainly not, not at all, not a bit." Haroun tried to calm her down. He had not bargained for hearing such words from a common servant when he had first come into the garden. "If you say so."

To his relief, the anger left her face. She began to laugh, although it was not a very jolly sound. "If I say so . . . But what am I saying? I forget who I am, now." Seeing how oddly Haroun was looking at her, she swiftly added, "I ask your forgiveness, O my Master. The poets and the story-tellers all agree that a broken heart often makes us act a little mad. I should not trouble you with my problems."

"Oh, I do not mind," Haroun replied, somewhat shyly. "A broken heart, you say?"

"Well ... I suppose it *ought* to be broken. My pride hurts, at any rate." Her brow wrinkled, and unexpectedly she demanded, "Have you ever thought you were in love?"

"Oh, yes, many ti——! That is, I understand what you mean." Haroun put on a solemn face and tried to seem older than he was. This was difficult, since now that he looked at her, he realized that the girl was about his age. "I assume that the boy you love does not love you?"

"Worse! He loves another. *Really* loves her, not just *thinks* he loves her. Do you understand that, as well?" Nur studied Haroun closely.

"Yes—that is—I mean—no." Haroun felt uncomfortable under Nur's steady gaze. There was something disturbing in this servant girl's eyes. It was the first time Haroun had really looked at her. How different this was from his enchanted princess! Oh, the enchanted princess had lovely eyes, true, but whenever Haroun spoke to her, they wandered. They were smiling eyes, eyes that looked back at him very prettily and politely, but there was nothing there behind them. It was like gazing into the eyes of one of his tame gazelles: beautiful, but boring.

Nur laughed again, and Haroun thought it was a very nice sound. He wondered how much nicer it might be if the girl were truly happy. "No, why should you understand? When you love, you love; there is no doubt in your heart or your mind about it, is there?"

Haroun said nothing. He was thinking about the servant girl's words. *Do I really love my enchanted princess?* He regarded Nur with new eyes. "Why did you love—*think* you loved him?" he asked.

Nur considered this. "Well, he is handsome. . . ." She let her eyes rest on Haroun's face. "But many men are handsome. And kind ... as are other men, too; not that I have met so many men in my life. In fact, he was the first I ever

99

met without someone at my back telling me I *ought* to love him."

The way the hero in all the old stories must always love a princess if he wants to live happily ever after, thought Haroun. Out loud he said, "Have you ever thought that what you loved was not him, but finally being free of all those *ought-to's*?"

Nur's mouth opened slightly in stunned admiration. "By all that is sacred, I think you have hit it, O my Master. Has anyone ever told you how wise you are?"

Haroun's chest puffed out, though he tried to act modest. "Oh, I am not so wise as all that, my dear." *What a smart girl!* he thought. "For example, if you can keep a secret I will tell you that I, too, have not made so many wise choices when it comes to love."

"You mean—my fellow servant?" Nur asked the question for form's sake. Lord Haroun's courtship of Tamar was the talk of the servants' quarters second only to Nur's pursuit of Khalid. "She is beautiful." Nur could not help sounding bitter when she said that.

"Beauty is not everything," Haroun replied, and surprised himself by meaning it. "It is too soon lost to age and time. If beauty is the only thing that makes you want to marry a person, what will you have left in the years after that beauty fades away?" A thought struck him like a thunderbolt, and he spoke it aloud: "Happily ever after is a very long time to be miserable."

This time Nur's laugh came from the heart, warming them both. "You are honest as well as wise, O my Master. I am grateful for honesty, even if it sometimes has sharp teeth. Let me return the favor and be honest with you, too. Do you see this ring?" She stuck out her right hand. The iron band was dull, but still seemed to glow in the garden sunlight.

Haroun studied the ring, holding Nur's hand to do so. He found this to be a very pleasing sensation and for a moment forgot why he was doing it. "It is—it is a very unusual piece of jewelry," he said. "A family gift?"

"A gift of magic," Nur confided. "I did not lie, you see, when I told you that magical beings serve me."

Haroun used all this concentration to keep his hand from shaking. It was very upsetting to hear this charming girl speak crazily again. "My dear—what *is* your name?"

"Nur."

"My dear Nur, how can you expect anyone to believe that? I am not saying it is impossible for you to have a little magic of your own—it is a free country for such things to happen, even to servants—but if you do have any magic at your command, why have you not—? Why are you still—?"

"Why am I working as a servant in this house?" Nur finished the question for him. Her fingers curled around his as she tilted her hand, the better to contemplate the iron ring. "Wish in haste, repent at leisure; and I have only one wish to my name."

"Really?" Haroun beamed at the thought of someone with but a single wish. "You are quite right, then; you must be extremely careful. How thrilling! How to wish for *just* what you want? How to make sure your genie does not trick you into wasting that wish? How exciting for you!"

"I think it is awful," Nur said. "I would rather be in your shoes, O my Master, with all the wishes I want."

"No, you do not." Haroun's face drooped with envy. "You just think you would like that. It is terribly dull, really. There is never any challenge. If I waste one wish, there are a dozen more where that came from—a hundred more! Wishes are not special for me anymore, and if magic becomes as common as radishes, what is the use of it?"

A sly look came into Nur's eyes. "If that is how you feel, O my Master, why do you not use one wish to rid yourself of all the rest?"

"What? Are you mad?" Haroun was scandalized. "Throw away wishes? Anyone who heard of it would think I was insane. How would I live, afterward? I am used to having everything I desire given to me at once. I am afraid I could never go back to things the way they were." Sadly, he let Nur's hand drop. "You could not understand."

"Oh, could I not?" Her brows rose. "You might be surprised. Before I came to work here, I was— Well, what I was then is unimportant. What matters is I too know that I could never go back to things the way they were. And yet, as un-

101

happy as I was then, there are times I think I could go back to that life . . . if I did not have to go back alone."

Haroun saw the way she looked at him when she said that. He grasped both her hands before he knew what he was doing. "You know, if you think you cannot decide what to use your one wish for, you might try wishing to be a princess. Being a princess has all sorts of advantages. You would be rich and have pretty clothes and live in a palace and—"

"I do not wish to be a princess," Nur said firmly.

"Oh." Haroun was downcast. "It was just a thought. Not a very good one. You do not look as if you would be comfortable, being a princess. I suppose it is something you have to be born to do right."

"Sometimes not even then," Nur remarked under her breath. More clearly she said, "Oh my Master, this ring I wear is also magical."

"I knew that," said Haroun. "It holds the genie who shall grant you your one wish, is it not so?"

"Oh, there is no genie in this old thing," Nur told him. The ring vibrated angrily on her finger, like an enraged bumblebee, but she did not notice. "But it does hold magic—the magic of eternal love." She repeated for him all that Gamal had told her about the ring, without mentioning how she had gotten it. She ended by saying, "My lord, you have been good to me. I know you love my friend—"

"Do you also then know that she does not love me?" Haroun asked. For some reason that thought did not make him as sorrowful as it might have. *If I want a princess so badly, I could have Khalid turn my girl into one,* he thought, eyes never leaving Nur's face.

"Hearts change," said Nur, pretending not to see the way he looked at her. "Perhaps hers will. You only have to have her say she loves you once, then give her this ring and she will love you always." She slipped it from her hand and pressed it into his. "There are all sorts of situations that might make a girl say she loves a boy."

Haroun's hand closed over Nur's. "Are there? Would you say—could you show me—can you—?"

"You are joking with me." Nur smiled at him fondly.

"Now I must go. I have work to do." She tried to leave the garden, but he would not release her hand.

"Hearts change, you say. Could yours—?"

"Oh, I know I said it was broken, but do not worry about me; it will mend." Her eyes twinkled. "It may heal faster than I thought." With a twist of her wrist she was free of his grasp and gone.

Haroun was left to stare at the iron ring in his palm.

You look just like a carp when you do that, the ring sneered. Its tiny voice went unheard.

12

Princess Nur went skipping through the halls of Lord Haroun's palace. Her heart felt lighter than it had in weeks. She was very pleased with herself and wanted nothing more than to find Tamar and tell the genie that she was ready to make her final wish.

She was so absorbed in happy thoughts that she did not see that cat Boabdil cross her path until she tripped over him. Boabdil let out an ear-splitting screech, even though he was unhurt. Nur picked him up at once and hugged him, which was just what he had intended. He let her pour out a thousand sweet names and apologies before he purred to show her all was forgiven.

"Oh, dear cat, please pardon me, but I was not thinking," Nur implored.

"You were not looking, either," Boabdil pointed out. "What could possibly distract you so?" He gave her a sidelong look. "Is it love?"

Nur promptly twirled the cat around and around the hall in a wild dance until he yowled. "Love? Yes, it is love, you darling cat! How very smart you are! How fine your fur! How glorious your whiskers! It is love, true love, and all the world is beautiful!"

"Put me down before I put my beautiful claws into your skin," Boabdil spat. When she did so, he ruffled up his fur at her. "So it is love. Even after Khalid told you he loves Tamar, you still insist on loving him? What a waste!"

"Love . . . Khalid?" Nur put her fingers to her lips and giggled.

"Where is the joke?" the cat asked, eyes flashing. There is nothing a cat hates worse than feeling as if he is on the wrong end of a cat-and-mouse match.

"This is a magical palace, cat," she said merrily. "A magical palace that has everything: not merely an enchanted princess—that's me, I suppose—and a pair of genies, but—can you keep the secret?—there is also a great and mighty wizard dwelling here."

"A wizard!" Boabdil hissed lightly. "That is all we need. Who let him in?"

"No one needed to," Nur replied. "He owns the palace, you see."

"Since when is Lord Haroun a wizard?" The cat switched his tail rapidly from side to side. "Since when is he anything but a silly, greedy boy with more toys than are good for him?" His golden eyes became suspicious slits. "Is *that* your riddle, lady? Is *he* the one you love?"

"Yes!" The word became a glad song on Nur's lips. "I was like the princess who slept for a hundred years, but now I am awake. In my dreams I thought I loved Khalid, but now, thanks to the wisdom of Lord Haroun, I know the truth."

"Wisdom?" Boabdil wiggled his ears. "Are you sure we are talking about the same Lord Haroun?"

"You do not know him," Nur said. "I did not know him either, until now. His wise words cleared my eyes; he let me see that I was being a stubborn child. I have spent so many years saying *no* to all the old kings my father wanted me to marry that saying *no* became a habit! Therefore, when Tamar asked me to have Haroun for my husband, I said *no* without thinking just because *no* is what I always say whenever I am asked to marry!" She folded her hands over her heart. "Dear cat, you must help me."

Boabdil gave the traditional feline reply: "If I feel like it. How?"

"You must help me decide how I can best use my last wish."

The cat flicked his ears forward, puzzled. "I thought that was settled. If you still love Lord Haroun—?"

"I do."

"Good. The way you mortals have been behaving, your hearts seem to flip over every few minutes, like griddle cakes. Then if you do love him, as you say, what is the problem? Wish to marry him, as my lady Tamar asked, and everything will be done and well done!"

Princess Nur shook her head. "I will not wish that wish."

"Why in the name of the great Moon Cat not?" Boabdil yowled, at the end of his patience.

"Because I think he loves me, too," Nur answered, her voice full of joy. "I could see it in his eyes; I could feel it in my heart. I will need no wish to make him marry me. Oh, Boabdil!" She knelt before the cat. "Can you imagine how happy he will be when he learns that his bride is a princess after all?"

"That will be quite a wedding present," the cat admitted. "But—what of the lifetime of wishes Tamar promised you if you wished for Haroun as a husband?"

A secret smile curved one corner of Nur's lips. "I think that it is time my dear Haroun learned that life may be lived quite comfortably without wishes. How can he learn that if I do not live the lesson myself? Let Tamar be free, Boabdil. Let Khalid, too, have his freedom at last. I will not open his prison only to lock her up in another one."

"You would do that for them?" For the first time in the history of all cats everywhere, a sane and healthy animal stared at a person with honest admiration in his eyes. "Are you *sure* you are a real human being?" Boabdil inquired skeptically.

Princess Nur laughed. "Real enough to ask your help about what to do with my remaining wish, dear cat! I would like it to be a wedding gift to Haroun, since it is the last wish either one of us will ever have, but I do not know what he would most enjoy."

"Well, what do you think he will be giving you?" the cat asked.

Nur's smile held a secret. "A ring," she said. "A plain iron ring, and that is all I desire."

"Hmmm. Iron, is it? I must say, either mortal brides'

taste in wedding gifts has changed or you are— Well, I am no longer certain about exactly *what* you are, my lady. But I like it. I will help you. I shall spy upon Lord Haroun and see if I can pick up any hints. Will that do?"

"That will do nicely," Nur scratched him behind the ears. "And I will go back into the kitchens to wait."

"For me?"

"For him; for Haroun. From what Tamar tells me, he will be coming along shortly to talk to me about . . . the weather." She sauntered off, singing again. Boabdil watched her go, flicked the air with his tail, and trotted away in the opposite direction to do as he had been asked.

Nur was almost to the kitchens when she suddenly skipped headfirst into a wall of solid air. Nothing was there to bar her path, yet she could not go a single step further. "What is this?" she wondered aloud, patting the invisible barrier with her hands.

A friend, said a familiar voice. *A friend who has come back to this palace to see how you are doing.*

"If you are my friend, show yourself!" Nur demanded.

You know the rules. The voice seemed to mock her. *Have you forgotten? You only need to call me by name.*

"Very well, if you insist." Nur was annoyed. "Show yourself, Gamal!"

The monstrous genie stood before her without any showy magical trimmings to accompany his appearance. This time he was solid, with legs instead of a trail of smoke, and no taller than an ordinary man. "I am here, my lady." His smile was cold and evil.

Nur was brave without knowing how brave she was; it was just in her to recognize a bully when she saw one and not to be afraid of him. "I do not see why that was necessary," she said. "If you wanted to see me, why did you not simply come?"

"Rules, my lady, as I said." Gamal bowed too deeply for the gesture to be anything but a nasty joke. "Have you ever heard me speak of the Council, whose laws command all genies everywhere? They are the ones who are so insistent that we follow their rules. They are very quick to punish us when we do anything wrong—even if the error is made for the best of reasons—and they become especially angry when someone interferes with one of their judgments."

"They sound like my father's advisers," Princess Nur said. "You can tell them anything except *You are wrong.*"

"I rejoice to hear that you and I share the same opinion of those old goats." Gamal's smile widened, showing off his tusks too much.

"You did not come here just for us to take turns insulting our elders." Nur was growing distinctly impatient with Gamal. "What do you want?"

Gamal put on a pained expression. "You hurt my feelings, my lady! I have only come back to fulfill my promise."

"The promise to help me make my last wish well?" Nur could not help beaming; she was too happy to hide her joy, even from Gamal. "If that is all, you may go. I already know what I shall use that wish for!"

"You do?" Gamal's black brows became a thundercloud above his yellow eyes. His keen sight narrowed on the princess's hands, and he saw . . . "Gone! The ring is gone! Then you have given it to him? Yes, you must have done it, or you would not be so happy. Oh, excellent!"

Nur tried to speak, but Gamal burst from his human-sized body into a towering pillar of sooty smoke that spun around her like a whirlwind. "He has the ring! He has it! Ha! Wonderful!" The genie's voice rumbled inside the spinning smoke with the might of an earthquake. Nur trembled in spite of herself and pressed her back against the wall while Gamal's wicked laughter made bits of the ceiling come tumbling down. "It is done, then! Soon it shall be over!"

The voice inside the whirlwind changed. Every word it spoke vibrated and glowed with great magic. "O Great Ones! O Wise Ones! O Ancient Ones, come at once to give your judgment and to punish the guilty one whom I have found!"

The walls of Lord Haroun's palace shook. A cold, wet wind blew through the rooms, smelling like old books left out in the rain. Nur's skin crept as if all the ants in the world were marching over it. She hugged herself tightly and wished she were not alone. Then, as if she had spoken that wish aloud, someone was standing beside her. She looked to her left and saw an old, old man. His hair was white, his skin was darker than the sun-browned skin of her father's best desert rider, and his eyes had the color and shine of rubies. Nur gasped. No human being could have such eyes. When he smiled, she saw that every tooth in his head was long and sharp as a dagger, and grassy green.

He was not the only one there. Four others stood behind him, each almost as old and hideous as he, each with cold, glittering red eyes. They were all dressed in silk and satin robes sewn with gold thread and dripping with precious jewels. Each one carried a lamp in his hands, but these were solid gold set with diamonds. Nur did not need anyone to tell her that she was about to meet the famous Council.

"Why have we been summoned?" the oldest-looking of the five ancient genies demanded. His voice creaked and cracked like a door on rusty hinges.

Gamal whisked away the dirty whirlwind and showed himself once more at human size. He knelt and touched his forehead to the floor. "O Great Ones, it was I, Gamal, who summoned you."

"Gamal . . . ?" The oldest genie scratched his head. "The name sounds familiar."

The youngest-looking of his companions tugged at his sleeve. "It was Gamal who called us before, when master Ishmael's prison was stolen."

"Ah, yes, that is it!" The oldest genie looked as pleased as if he had remembered it by himself. Turning to Gamal he demanded, "And where is Master Ishmael's prison, Gamal? Return it to us at once!"

With his face still on the floor, Gamal replied, "O Ancient One, you speak as if it were I who stole the prison in the first place. Can you believe I would commit such a crime?" (Nur had a chilly, certain feeling in her stomach that it would take far less time to list the crimes Gamal would *not* commit, but she said nothing.) "Yet a crime *has* been committed, I admit. Allow me now the honor of bringing the guilty one before you for punishment!"

The oldest genie wrinkled his brow. "You know who the criminal is?"

"You will find him within the walls of this humble

building, O Wise One." Gamal dared to raise his head a bit and smile a foxy smile. "Shall I name his name?"

"Are we, then, powerless?" The oldest genie glared at Gamal scornfully. "We need no more from you than you have already given us." He raised the hand in which he carried his gold lamp and in a voice to make the thunder flee he boomed, "LET THEM COME!"

Earlier Nur had wished for company, and now she had it. The magical command of the oldest member of the Council was enough to fetch every living, breathing creature in Lord Haroun's palace. Lord Haroun himself was there, and Boabdil the cat. Khalid and Tamar, still in her mortal disguise, appeared together, holding hands as if that was what they had been doing at the moment they were summoned. Three female and five male servants whom Nur had never seen before stared in terror at the five magnificent genies before dropping their brooms and dustcloths and racing away, screaming.

"Let them run," Gamal said quickly, jumping to his feet. "You want none of them, O Great Ones. Nor him." He pointed at old Yazid, who stood leaning on a rake and blinking at the Council. "Go away, old man."

Old Yazid shook his rake at Gamal. "I will go when I am good and ready, you young puppy!" Gamal twitched one finger, and the floor between them swarmed with an army of fat, black, hairy spiders. "Now—now I am ready," the old fellow stammered, and ran after the other servants as if he were thirty years younger.

Gamal was so eager, he did not bother ordering anyone else out. He strode across the floor, growing bigger with every step, until by the time he reached Khalid his head brushed the ceiling. "Here he is, O Great Ones!" he shouted in triumph. "Here is the one you want, the thief, the one who stole my poor Master Ishmael's prison!"

"Thief?" Tamar cried, holding tight to Khalid. "You are crazy, Gamal. How can you say—?"

"Be silent," the oldest genie commanded. He did not even have to raise his voice. Tamar knew who he was and knew that it would only hurt Khalid to argue with any member of the Council. She bowed to him and said no more.

But Khalid had something to say for himself. "Master Ishmael in prison? My beloved teacher, punished? What for?" He was so appalled by this news that he did not bother to defend himself against Gamal's accusation.

The youngest member of the Council noticed this and came over to pat Khalid on the shoulder. "There, there. It is good to see such affection for a teacher. A very *good* teacher, I think he was, but he lacked judgment. We were sent a message telling us that he gave one of his students a lamp, right away, instead of making him work his way up from a magic ring or a brass bottle or an enchanted spicebox. We were also told that the results were . . ." He looked embarrassed. "Well, they were nothing for genies to be proud of."

By this time, Nur had gotten over her fear of the Council. They really did remind her of her father's advisers—old men who had held her on their laps since she was a child and who laughed at everything she said, even when she was being serious. She did not like them at all. "Tell me, O Great One," she spoke up boldly. "Who was it that told you about this—*mistake* of Master Ishmael's?"

"Who told. . . ?" The youngest Council member thought about it. "Why, I believe the letter was not signed."

"I thought so," said Nur, giving Gamal a meaningful look. "And I also think that believing an unsigned letter of accusation is also nothing for genies to be proud of."

"Who are you, to tell us how we should think?" the oldest genie growled.

"No one! She is no one!" Haroun rushed to Nur's side and stood between her and the furious genie. "She is only Nur, one of my servants. Do not harm her! Good servants are so hard to find." He raised his right hand, as if that could stop the powers of five of the mightiest genies.

"THE PRISON!" The oldest genie's red eyes flashed. Sparks flew from them and landed on the iron ring, which Haroun had placed on the third finger on his right hand. Haroun let out a startled yelp as the ring flew from his finger and clattered to the floor. "He is the thief!"

"Thief? Me?" Haroun crossed his now-bare hands over his heart. "Why would I want to steal an imprisoned genie?"

"To free him, of course!" The oldest genie's eyes became

hard red slits glowing like eternal fires. "What mortal does not possess the power to free a genie, even one whom we, the Council, have imprisoned?"

"To free him," said the next-youngest genie, "and then to claim his magic."

"To free him," said the next in line, "before his allotted time of punishment is over."

"To free him," said the third, "and by doing so to fly in the face of our judgment."

"Look at him!" The oldest genie's lip curled in scorn. "Look at that shocked expression he has put on like a badly made mask. Yet even if he were a good actor, there is no arguing with the fact that he had Master Ishmael's prison in his possession. There is no doubt or question: he is the thief."

"*He!*" Gamal's mouth fell open like a poorly latched trapdoor.

"Why are you so surprised?" asked the youngest member of the Council, who often noticed things his elders did not. "I thought you said you knew who it was."

"Yes, but—I thought—he is not supposed to be—"

"ENOUGH!" The oldest genie threw his arms wide and shot up from human size until he shattered the ceiling of the hall. Without thinking, Tamar and Khalid threw a spell of shielding over Nur and Haroun, an umbrella of white light that protected the two humans from tumbling bricks and falling plaster. Boabdil the cat looked after himself, diving under the robes of the oldest genie.

That ancient creature was so furious that he did not notice or care if a cat was sharing his clothing. Rage made his face turn crimson. He leveled a huge finger at Haroun, and his words fell like lead. "I know your name without anyone to tell it to me, Haroun ben Hasan. Why does it not surprise me to learn that it was you who stole Master Ishmael's prison? It is not enough for you to hold one genie captive—you must have two! O mortal man, your greed is a legend among us. Your name is taught in the schoolrooms as a lesson with which to frighten young genies and as a constant reminder to all of us that mortal men are never to be trusted."

"Now just one moment—" Haroun protested.

"One moment will not be enough for you to think about your greed. Take several!" The oldest genie's hands shot purple and crimson stars. One struck Haroun on the forehead and he began to dissolve into smoke from the feet up, as if he himself were a genie returning to his lamp. Nur grabbed his hands, only to have them trickle away between her fingers as the unhappy young man was drawn into the center of the iron ring on the floor. He vanished with a little sigh.

Princess Nur wasted no time on tears. "What have you done to him?" she shrieked, her face white as bone. She faced the Council in a truly royal rage. "Speak, you herd of old goats! *What have you done?*"

She did not wait for an answer. Teeth clenched, hands balled into fists, she threw herself to her knees before Tamar. "Hear my last wish well, O my good friend and servant!" she cried. "Grant it, and then take your freedom. *I wish that I might never part from Haroun ben Hasan, no matter the peril, no matter the price!*"

"But—but—" Tamar tried to bring Nur to her feet. "But you know nothing of where he has gone or when—*if*—he shall ever emerge. Would you not rather—?"

"I would rather be with one I love, even in a prison of iron, than without him in the palace of a king. Grant my wish, O genie." Nur looked steadily into Tamar's eyes. "Grant it now."

Tamar saw she had no choice. Tears flowed from her eyes, but she managed to say what was expected of her: "Hearkening and obedience."

Tamar's magic was not as showy as the oldest genie's. There were no bright stars or any sound of thunder. The wish simply *happened*. The genies watched as Princess Nur dwindled into a wisp of smoke that poured itself into the iron ring. Her expression never changed: calm and sure of her decision, she went to join Haroun ben Hasan with a serene and joyful smile.

13

"**W**ell, my boy, how does it feel to be free at last?" the youngest genie of the Council asked, patting Khalid on the back.

"Not as good as I thought it would." Khalid did not look at him. He was still staring at the iron ring. So was Tamar. He could see her shoulders shaking, and he knew without seeing the tears that she was crying.

"Free?" Gamal could not keep the indignation out of his voice. "What do you mean, he is free?"

The oldest genie explained it for him: "By attempting to get a second genie while he still had one working for him, Haroun ben Hasan forfeited his right to own any genie at all, now or ever." Looking smug, he added, "The closest he shall ever come to another genie is Master Ishmael, for Haroun ben Hasan is hereby condemned to share Master Ishmael's prison for as long as that genie remains in the iron ring."

"And for how long is that?" Khalid asked.

"Oh, a trifle," the youngest genie said happily. "His mistake was so small. Just a hundred years."

"Give or take a decade for good behavior," said the second-eldest.

"But that is terrible!" Khalid protested. "Nothing Lord Haroun has done was bad enough to deserve such a punishment."

"Do not tell the Council what is and is not a proper

punishment," the oldest genie menaced, "or perhaps we will practice our judgments on you."

Khalid stood tall and fearlessly faced the ancient creature. "Even though you threaten me, still I will speak: Lord Haroun may have been greedy, but he was poor when he found me. It is frightening for a mortal to be poor. He saw me as his chance never to be poor again, and he took it. It was *my* responsibility to protect him from his fear, and it was *my* mistake that made Lord Haroun such a grasping man. Must he lose a century of freedom for that? You forget that mortals do not have the same lifespans we do. When he emerges from the ring, he shall crumble to dust! No, he should not suffer for my error; I should."

"O wisdom!" Gamal cried, clapping his hands and grinning with evil glee. "Heed him, O Great Ones! For once Khalid knows what he is talking about."

The Council did not hear Gamal, or else ignored him.

"Do not worry about the mortal Haroun ben Hasan," said the third-eldest genie.

"He will be the same age when he comes out of the ring as he was when he went in," said the fourth.

"And what of Nur, who is my Master?" asked Tamar, her face wet.

"Hmph!" The oldest genie snorted. "Silly creature. Never in all my eons as a genie have I ever heard a wish like the one *she* made. She will be the same, too, I suppose."

"She may and he might, but what of the world?" Khalid exclaimed. "Will that, also, be the same when they come out?"

"What a question! Of course not." The oldest genie shrugged. "What does it matter?"

"To you, nothing." Tamar's eyes were dry now, and stared hard at the leader of the Council. "But to a human being, much." Without another word, she snapped herself into a spear of smoke and plunged into the center of the iron ring.

"To you, nothing," Khalid repeated. "But to those who have lived with humans long enough to think of them as friends, it matters a great deal." He too turned to smoke and dived after Tamar.

The Council and Gamal gazed at the iron ring for a long while, too stunned to speak. Then the youngest genie said, "I wonder if we might not have made a little mistake, gentlemen. If this Haroun ben Hasan was so wicked a Master, why would Khalid speak so strongly in his defense? Why would he speak of humans as friends?"

"Because Khalid is a fool and has always been a fool," Gamal spat. He glared at the ring. "Who else but a fool would defend a human?"

The youngest genie looked at Gamal narrowly. "We never did find out who sent us that message about Master Ishmael, did we?" he remarked casually.

"Why do you stare at me like that?" Gamal demanded. "I will not stand for it!"

The oldest genie reached into one of his sleeves and drew out a much-folded piece of paper. "No, we did not," he said. "But by good luck, I have the message here with me. I never throw anything away." He seemed proud of the fact. "We could still cast the proper spells of discovery, if you think it is important."

"The mortal girl thought it was important," said the youngest genie.

"The mortal girl is a bigger fool than that empty-headed Haroun, and he is a worse fool than Khalid, and Tamar is the greatest fool of them all!" Gamal shrieked. He waved his hands and his own lamp appeared. Before any of the Council could do a thing, he lifted the lid of his lamp, grabbed up the iron ring, and dropped it inside. With a terrible laugh of victory and a blazing blast of orange flames, Gamal vanished.

The youngest genie reached for the lamp. A crackle of blue sparks burned his fingers badly. "How could I be so stupid?" he said, shaking them. "A genie's lamp is his castle. No other genie may enter it unless he is asked."

"Nor leave it unless a mortal frees him," the second-oldest genie added.

The other two genies just looked at each other and remarked, "Oh, dear."

"But the prison is in there!" the oldest Council member objected. "Khalid and Tamar are inside! They can get out of the ring whenever they like, because they are not being punished, but they cannot escape from Gamal's lamp. What does he mean to do with them?"

The hem of the ancient genie's robe rippled. Boabdil the cat stuck his nose out, sniffed the air for danger, then emerged and trotted over to the lamp. He sniffed this too before saying, "Well, I do not think he will invite them to a sherbet party." He sat down and looked at the Council. "O Wise Ones, when you make a mistake, it is a beauty."

Inside the iron ring, Khalid finally caught up with Tamar after what felt like hours. She was flying down the seemingly endless curved corridor when he grabbed the wispy end of her robes and forced her to stop. She looked so surprised to see him that he said, "Well? Did you think I would let you come after them alone?"

Tamar's smile lit up the dingy gray interior. "I am glad to have your help." She offered him her hand. "I think we two must be the only genies in the universe who believe human beings are worth looking after."

"Then we must stay together, so that we do not share such dangerous beliefs with other genies." Khalid's hand closed over hers, and for the first time in his life he looked truly happy. "With humans, it is only a matter of understanding them. I would even dare to say that they are not so different from us. Lord Haroun and I would often have some very interesting talks between wishes, and he did not *have* to hire human servants to help me around the palace. A good heart cannot hide itself forever."

"How true," Tamar agreed. "My Master, the Princess Nur, is also very easy to get along with." She looked around at their grim surroundings and shuddered. "I only hope that she will be as easy to find."

"I do not think that finding her will be that hard," Khalid said. "This is a ring, after all. It just goes around."

"And around and around and around," said Tamar. "If Nur and Haroun are going in the same direction as we are and they keep walking, we might not catch up with them."

"Then we shall not walk, my lady," Khalid floated up from the iron floor, taking Tamar with him. "We shall fly."

And fly they did. It was one of the most boring flights either one of them had ever known. The inside of the ring never changed. It was always the same dull gray all around them. Before long the two genies discovered a rule that human beings had known for ages: boredom makes time stretch itself out like a piece of taffy.

"How long have we been flying?" Tamar asked.

"Days," Khalid replied with a groan. "Months. Maybe years. Who knows?" He landed lightly and sat down on the hard, curved floor. "Perhaps we acted too hastily, Tamar. What can we do for Haroun and Nur if we do find them? He is condemned to remain in this prison for a hundred years and she, by her own wish, can never leave him. We cannot get them out of here."

"Why, we can—we can protect them," Tamar answered.

"Protect them from what?"

Tamar landed too, sat beside Khalid, and looked around. She saw only gray emptiness and more gray emptiness. "The Council did say this was a prison, and I thought they might have done something to the inside to discourage any genie from trying to break in and free Master Ishmael. You know: bottomless swamps, trackless deserts, hideous monsters."

"Such obstacles are not necessary. What genie would dare try to free Master Ishmael, knowing that the Council would find out about it sooner or later?" Khalid sighed. "A hideous monster would at least liven this place up a little."

Thank you very much, I am sure, but I happen to think the place looks quite lively enough the way I have it fixed up now! The voice boomed through the endless iron corridor, making the walls quiver. Tamar shrieked and threw herself into Khalid's arms.

"What is it? What is it?" she gasped, her eyes squeezed shut.

"How should I know?" he wailed, his eyes just as tightly closed as hers.

Really, my children, the voice spoke again, *I expected a kinder greeting than this. I have never meant anyone any harm. Look at me. I have missed you.*

Very cautiously Khalid and Tamar opened their eyes. The dull gray corridor was gone. Instead they found themselves seated on a thick, grassy lawn beside an ivory fountain. A little way off was a forest of slender, elegant trees where pheasants and red deer walked. Right where the grass met the forest was a silk tent, white with stripes of blue and gold. A simple blue banner with a silver cup on it flew from the top of the center pole.

From inside the tent, the voice called, *Come in! Come in! We are waiting for you.*

"Oh!" Tamar cried gladly. "I know that voice now!"

"So do I," Khalid exclaimed. The two of them ran a race to be the first into the tent and wound up tripping over each other at the entrance. As they lay sprawled on the fine carpet, they heard familiar laughter.

"Khalid, a man is known by the genie he keeps. I wish you would not embarrass me like that." Lord Haroun coughed, then added, "Oh, did I say *wish*? Sorry. Force of habit."

Khalid got up and helped Tamar to her feet. He saw his former Master seated on a chair fit to be a king's throne, with the Princess Nur on another one beside him. A copper table laden with all kinds of food and drink was set up before them, and behind them stood Master Ishmael.

"You see?" Khalid's old teacher said, gesturing to show off the tent and everything outside it. "I do not think that I have done such a bad job of making my prison a little bit more comfortable."

"Indeed it is so, Master Ishmael," said Khalid, admiring all the wonderful things the tent held. There were intricately embroidered hangings between the many tent poles, each telling part of King Solomon's story. The floor was covered with fat cushions and brilliantly colored carpets; in the very center, a tiny silver fountain shot a spray of rose perfume into the air. Yet in spite of all these marvels, the one object that attracted Khalid's attention was a plain, unadorned sword that hung by its hilt from a leather thong above the silver fountain. The thong itself was tied to thin air. "Is this—? Can this be—?" Khalid breathed, gazing at the sword.

"It is," Master Ishmael replied solemnly. "The very sword of Solomon himself. I was permitted to take it with me into my prison as a special favor of the Council."

Nur laughed. "If all prisons were like this one, we would be overrun with criminals."

Master Ishmael frowned at her. "Do not be deceived, my child. My humble magic powers have allowed me to create all that you see, yet they are not enough to let me see this place as anything but a prison. I know that I am not free. The strongest bars are those which stand around my heart."

"True," said Nur. "Yet I cannot ever think of this place as a prison, even though I must stay here for a hundred years." She reached out and took Haroun's hand. "Where he is, I am; I need no other freedom."

"Nor do I," said Haroun. He smiled at Master Ishmael and added, "Of course I do not mind having all this lime-and-pecan sherbet, too." He waved at the icy bowls on the copper table.

"Lime and pecan?" Khalid sprang for it, passed Tamar a chilled cup, and soon they were all seated on cushions around the table, smacking their lips over Master Ishmael's bounty. "This is very nice," Khalid remarked some time later, licking his spoon clean. "But still that does not change the fact that Tamar and I have come to get you all out of here."

"How?" Master Ishmael asked. "The Council—"

"I will make the Council see that you are not to be blamed for what happened," Khalid replied. "If they need a prisoner, I will tell them that they can have me."

Tamar leaned near and put her arms around him. "And me. You shall not spend the century alone."

Oh, yes he shall!

A fierce wind tore through the entrance of the tent, ripping away part of the silk. Outside the red deer ran off, bellowing in terror as the lovely trees were torn up by the roots. The pheasants took to the air, only to have the magnificent feathers stripped from their bodies by the black blast. The grass withered and died.

Purple and green fire fell on the roof of the tent, burning it away. Solomon's sword swayed at the end of its tether. The gigantic face of Gamal peered down at them, yellow eyes cold with hate. *You are all my prisoners now,* he gloated. The words ached in their ears even though he never moved his lips. *This pitiful little prison now lies inside my own lamp. Even if the Council says that you are free, none of you may leave without my permission.*

Nur turned to Tamar and whispered, "Is this true?"

Tamar nodded grimly. "A genie is master of everything inside his own lamp. No magical creature can enter or escape it unless he allows, and even he cannot emerge from the lamp without a mortal to release him." Her mouth looked hard. "Gamal must hate us very much for him to have followed us this far."

I heard that, Tamar, the ugly genie cried. *Hate you? No. There is only one I hate.* His face seemed to shoot flaming arrows into Khalid's heart. *I have hated too long, but that will end soon. Come out, Khalid, and fight me. I challenge you to a duel of magic. Once it is done and you are destroyed, you have my word that I will tell the Council to set the others free.*

"I am not afraid of you," Khalid said, getting to his feet. "And I do not think that I shall be the one who is destroyed." He started for the tattered doorway, but Tamar clung to him and made him stop.

"Do not go!" she exclaimed. "I do not trust his word any more than a snake's."

Harsh words. Gamal's voice boomed inside their heads, his nasty chuckling sounding like great waves battering the shore. *Why doubt me, Tamar?*

"Because the truth that will free these prisoners is the same truth that will make the Council lock you away in their place," she replied.

So it is. Yet I will not mind my prison as long as I have you to share it with me.

Tamar shook her head in disbelief. "You are insane."

I am not. It is your word, not mine, that shall free the prisoners. Gamal leered down at her. *Give your promise that you will stay with me for as long as the Council keeps me prisoner, and I will tell them the truth of who betrayed Master Ishmael, who stole the iron ring, and how it came to be on Haroun ben Hasan's hand.*

"You will tell them the truth without any promise from

her!" Khalid shouted. "I will see to that." He shook himself free of Tamar's arms and strode out of the tent.

Gamal clicked his tongue, and a pitying smile twisted its way over his huge face. *This will not take long.* The face vanished. An instant later the whole tent rocked with the shock of a mighty explosion.

14

They rushed from the tent in time to see two towers of flame collide. One was the color of ashes and charred wood, the other flashing silver and spring-green. The air stank so terribly that the humans covered their noses and mouths with their hands and still choked and coughed horribly. Every bit of the artificial sunlight that Master Ishmael had conjured up to brighten his prison seemed to have been sucked away. In the dreadful gloom, the two genies battled.

The dark fire peeled itself away and changed into the shape of a dragon with eyes of bronze and talons as long as lances. It slashed at the green-and-silver flame with teeth and claws, then bathed it in a stream of poisonous smoke from its terrible mouth. The brighter fire shrank back, but only for a moment. Then it took a new shape too, standing tall against the gray sky as a griffon, with the strength of a lion in its body and the majestic power of an eagle in its head and wings. It leaped into the air and dived at the dragon, making the beast scream and cower with fear.

But when the griffon tried to soar away for a second attack, the dragon changed into a serpent and lashed itself around the griffon's hind legs, dragging it down. The griffon struggled for a moment, then appeared to melt away. It was a stream of green-and-silver water that slipped easily through the serpent's coils and soaked into the ground.

Gamal twisted this way and that, frustrated and enraged to have lost Khalid. His mouth gaped, showing icy fangs that dripped venom. His fury was so great that he looked ready to bite himself. Then his rage discovered a new target. His flat head swung slowly around and his lidless black eyes fixed themselves on the humans. With a loud hiss, he flung himself at Haroun and Nur.

Thick stalks of silver-and-green bamboo thrust themselves out of the earth between the snake and the mortals. Each stem was thicker than a man's leg and hard as iron. The snake hit the rustling wall headfirst and reeled back, stunned. Shadows in the bamboo shifted, showing a fuzzy outline of Khalid's laughing face. A vine noose shot out of the thicket and tried to snare the giant serpent while he was still groggy.

Gamal was too quick for it. He kept his shape, but shrunk himself down to snakeling size and slithered through the noose. Quick as thought, he glided into the heart of the bamboo wall, curled himself around a single stem, and tried to sink his fangs into it.

The bamboo became a ghost, the snakeling's fangs snapped shut on nothing. Music filled the iron prison, music that made the curved walls and floor vibrate strongly. The snakeling could not see his enemy, and because snakes have no ears, Gamal could not hear the music that Khalid had become. He could not hear it, but before long he began to feel it. The vibrations grew more powerful. The many notes of the music became a single tone, like the chiming of a great brass bell. Nur and Haroun felt it, too, and even the genies Tamar and Master Ishmael had to cover their ears as the note droned on, louder and louder.

At first the vibration was only enough to make the snakeling Gamal feel uneasy without knowing why. The floor under his belly hummed, and the humming spread into his body little by little. Gamal shook, and the swelling note seemed likely never to stop until it had shaken his fragile snakeling bones apart. He tried to change shape, but by the time he had noticed what was going on, he was trapped by the sound, his mind too full of panic to concentrate on working any magic. His small mouth hung open, his forked tongue drooped, and with a last, weak hiss, he toppled over, limp and motionless.

The note stopped. The iron ring no longer vibrated.

Flakes of color fell from the air and became Khalid. Tamar ran to him with a happy cry.

"Well done," said Master Ishmael, bowing to his favorite student.

Nur squeezed Haroun's hand. "I am so glad that is over," she said.

Haroun was still staring at the body of the snakeling. Silently he made Nur release his hand, then went into the ruined tent. He returned an instant later with the sword of Solomon and marched right over to where Gamal lay. "My father did not leave me much money when he died," he said, "but he did leave me plenty of good advice. 'My son,' he would say, 'never trust a dead snake until you have cut off its head.' " He raised the sword.

A wise man, your father! The snakeling's body split apart and Gamal sprang forth. He snatched the sword of Solomon from Haroun's hands effortlessly and tossed it far away from him. Everyone could hear his words in their thoughts. *It will take more than a tune to destroy me, Khalid,* he gloated, *but I think it will take much less to get rid of this human creature.*

"Let him go, Gamal!" Khalid shouted. "The duel is done; I won fairly."

Gamal spoke aloud, saying: "Fine; if you win, he loses. There is still time to surrender."

"It is not fair!" Nur stamped her foot, fists clenched. "He *did* win! Why should he give in to you?"

"I never said he *had* to give in." Gamal grinned and moved his hands so that they could all see how close his talons lay to Haroun's neck. "Khalid has his choice to make; I have mine."

"You horrid liar!" Nur was so angry, she spoke her mind without stopping to think about whether it was wise to call Gamal names while he held Haroun hostage. "When you told me about all the rules you genies must obey, you lied like a camel-seller! Where are your famous rules now?"

"Rules are for fools," Gamal sneered. "Oh, I follow them, but only when those old Council crows are there to keep an eye on me. Otherwise I do what I like, and that bunch of doddering fossils are never any the wiser."

"Ohhh, you—you—*you*—!" Nur's face was getting very red. She seethed like a boiling kettle as she searched for just the right words to tell Gamal how low and hateful and repulsive she thought he was. She was so angry that no name seemed terrible enough to call him, and the rage bottled up inside her made her feel ready to explode. Then, when she thought she would burst, the whisper of a thought crept into her mind:

My, my. Do you not just wish that the Council themselves were here to listen to what Gamal thinks of them?

"Yes!" Nur cried aloud. "Yes, I certainly *do* wish the Council were here and knew what you just said about them!"

"Hearkening and obedience," said Tamar.

A hand heavy with rage and authority fell on Gamal's shoulder. Another closed around his wrist, making him free Haroun. Two more got behind him and shoved, while a slippered foot stuck itself out in front of him and made him trip. By the time a stunned Gamal picked himself off the floor, the five members of the Council were standing around him in a circle.

"Crows, eh?" The oldest genie's ruby eyes were colder and harder than usual.

"Doddering fossils, are we?" the youngest asked.

"Rules are for fools, you say?" The second oldest tapped his foot.

"You only follow them when we are watching, do you?" The third oldest smiled, but it was not a comforting smile.

"My dear colleague, why should he do otherwise?" the fourth oldest pointed out. "We are never any the wiser. *Are* we?" His grin was even more frightening than his friend's.

"Gamal, your evil is at an end," the oldest Council member intoned. "We have discovered that it was you who accused Master Ishmael, and now we see that you did it not to serve justice, but only to serve yourself."

"What is more," the youngest genie chimed in, "you stole your old teacher's prison for some wicked reason. Of this we are sure, although how Haroun ben Hasan got it—"

"Gamal stole it and gave it to me!" Princess Nur declared.

All five members of the Council scowled at her. "Be quiet, human," said the oldest genie. "We do not need your help in taking care of our problems."

Still brave as ever, Nur replied, "If not for my wish, you never would have known Gamal's true opinion of you! He is a liar and a cheat." She told them of the false tales Gamal had told her about the iron ring and its powers. "Now I know that he hoped I would give it to Khalid, so that he would get the blame for stealing it."

"And so he would have," Gamal snarled, "if you humans were not so unreliable when it comes to love!"

"It may take us a while to make up our minds," Nur answered, "but once we decide, we do not need any magic rings to keep our love true." She stretched out her hand, and Haroun ran to take it. He stood proudly by her side as she said, "There is yet another crime to add to Gamal's list. When he first appeared, he tried to make me let *him* say how I would use my last wish. I can just imagine what sort of trick he would have played if I had been silly enough to let him do that!"

"One genie interfering with the wishes granted by another?" The oldest Council member frowned. "That is serious. Her last wish, too. Why, if she had wasted that, she would never have been able to wish to be with this fine young mortal forever, and then we might never have learned—"

"In the sacred names of magic and mathematics, hold!"

The iron ring shook. The youngest genie held up four fingers that shone like summer stars in the gloom. "Each genie learns to grant no more than three wishes to each mortal served. Accidents happen, but not frequently. Rules exist, and only *real* fools think they can get away without obeying them. This girl used her last wish to follow Haroun ben Hasan, yet she had a fourth wish granted to bring us here. Who did it? Who gave her a wish that was not hers to have?" His accusing stare went from Gamal, to Khalid, to Tamar, and there it stayed.

Tamar bowed her head. "Punish me for that," she said.

"So we will," the oldest genie said, "as soon as we are

all out of here. You, too, Master Ishmael. The rest of your sentence is hereby forgiven. Gamal shall have this fine prison all to himself for a thousand years!"

"Give or take a century for good behavior," the youngest genie put in. "Let us be gone!" The Council joined hands while Tamar and Khalid took hold of Haroun and Nur, ready to fly from the iron prison.

Nothing happened.

Gamal snickered. "At least I will not lack company for those thousand years."

"What does this mean?" Haroun demanded.

"Alas, we forgot." The youngest genie hung his head. "Gamal threw the iron ring into his own lamp, and that is a prison no genie may escape unless a mortal summons him out."

"Well, then I suppose we must wait for someone to rub the lamp." Nur did not seem to be worried about it. "That should not take too long."

"Oh no?" Gamal showed all his teeth nastily. "Every mortal in Haroun ben Hasan's palace was scared away. Even now I will bet that they are telling the whole city that the palace is haunted, a place of great and evil magic. No one will dare to go inside. No one will find the lamp. No one will be brave enough to touch it, let alone rub it." He stretched out on the bare iron floor as if it were the softest couch. "We are all in here for a good long time."

"I doubt that," said a soft, rumbly voice from above. A sudden shaft of light fell over all the prisoners. They looked up, but the light was too dazzling for them to see anything.

"Oh!" Tamar exclaimed. "Oh, do you feel that?" Her hand tightened on Nur's.

"What is it? What is it?" the princess demanded. All the genies except Gamal had their eyes closed and their faces tilted up into the light.

"It is—it feels like—ah, do not ask me to describe it!" Khalid gasped. "No human could ever understand."

"The lamp!" The oldest genie's voice lost all the hardness of age as if some very strange and wonderful force were

making him as young as Khalid again. "Someone is rubbing the lamp!"

"No!" Gamal bellowed. "It is not possible!"

"Possible or not, it is happening," the youngest genie beamed. He began to rise. Higher and higher he went, until he was pulled through the iron roof of the ring. One by one the others followed, first the Council, then Tamar, then Nur, then Khalid, and finally—

"Wait a moment!" Haroun let go of Khalid and scurried away. He came running back with the sword of Solomon just in time to grab the genie's hand and be lifted up.

"No, no, *no!*" Gamal lay alone in the circle of light and pounded the floor with fists and feet. "This cannot be! Nobody was left in the palace! Nobody could possibly rub the lamp and set them free!"

"Be careful whom you call a nobody," said the cat Boabdil, and used his nose to slam down the lid of Gamal's lamp, leaving the wicked genie in darkness.

15

The oldest genie brushed imaginary wrinkles out of his robe and cleared his throat importantly. The first thing that the Council had done once they were out of Gamal's lamp was to confer about Tamar's punishment for granting extra wishes. Now they were ready, and Tamar waited nervously to hear what they had to say.

Khalid refused to leave her side. "Whatever they decide to do to you, they will have to do to me, too," he promised.

"They will not do anything to her," Haroun declared, raising the sword of Solomon. "I will not allow it. If she had not granted Nur's fourth wish, they never would have known about Gamal."

The oldest genie glowered at him. "Put that down. If you want to scare a genie, you need the right kind of magic. The only spell on that old thing is one that will make you win any fight against other humans. I would not advise trying it out on us."

"Oh," said Haroun. He let the sword fall slowly to his side.

"And now, Tamar, hear the decision of the Council!" The oldest genie's words filled Lord Haroun's palace like the pounding hoofbeats of a herd of warhorses. Tamar fell to her knees and hid her face. Khalid knelt beside her, his expression a mixture of helplessness, anger, and love.

"I *wish* you would not shout like that," said the cat Boabdil. "In fact, I *wish* you would not say anything at all until I give you permission."

The oldest genie opened his mouth. Nothing came out.

"Oh, good," said Boabdil. "It worked even without him saying 'Hearkening and obedience.' But of course, how could he say anything after what I wished? The best sort of magic is the kind that makes sense." He swished his tail and rubbed against the oldest genie's ankles. "I will save the last wish *you* owe me to allow you to speak again, never fear." He then faced the other genies. "Hmmm, four plus Master Ishmael plus Khalid plus—no, no, I cannot claim any from Tamar. . . . Well, that is still six genies at three wishes each or—" Boabdil closed one eye in concentration. "I *wish* I were better at mathematics."

"Hearkening and obedience!" the youngest genie blurted out, then looked as stunned as if a stranger had just borrowed his mouth.

"Eighteen!" Boabdil exclaimed, overjoyed at his new talent. "Take away the one wish you just granted," he added, addressing the youngest Council member. "Still, seventeen wishes are nothing for any cat worth his fur to sneeze at."

"What has happened? What wishes? What has this small beast done? What does he mean by this?" Those Council members who could speak all spoke at once until the air was thick with unanswered questions.

"I *wish* you would pay attention!" Boabdil snapped at them, and instantly they did so. "Hmph. Only sixteen wishes left, but it was worth it. Now listen: I freed you from the lamp. Do I need to tell you what you owe me for that little favor?"

"Three wishes," said the second-oldest genie reluctantly.

"Apiece, it seems," said the third-oldest.

"But *only* three apiece!" the fourth-oldest pointed out.

"Certainly," Boabdil purred. "You did not even have to make that rule clear to me. All cats know that enough is enough. Greed is for humans and other creatures who were unlucky enough not to be born feline."

All the genies except Tamar bowed to the cat, and all the genies except Tamar and the silenced oldest Council member asked, "What is your wish, O Master?"

As usual it was the youngest who noticed things.

"Tamar, you were freed from the lamp like the rest of us. Why do you not bow before our new Master?"

"She cannot," the cat replied for her.

"Why not? She was in the lamp with us!"

"Tsk. I thought you knew your own business better than that." Boabdil preened his whiskers. "Can any genie obey a new Master while she still serves the old?"

"The old? but she has already granted the mortal girl three wishes!" the youngest genie objected. "No, *four!*"

"And she shall grant more, if her Master desires," Boabdil said. "I *wish* that you would all know why."

"Hearkening and obedience!" cried Khalid. He flung his hands high, and the ceiling overhead became a swirl of clouds. A gentle wind blew the mists aside and everyone saw the faces of Princess Nur and Tamar in a vision out of the past.

. . . and if you will have Lord Haroun ben Hasan for your husband, Tamar's image was saying, *then I shall grant you all the wishes you may ever desire. I swear it by the wisdom of King Solomon, by the skill of my own magic, and by the power of the great Council.*

The vision disappeared. "I am now down to fifteen wishes," said the cat. "I hope that I will not have to use any more of them to make you understand."

"So Tamar did promise this girl extra wishes from the start. A promise is a promise," the second-oldest genie admitted.

"But the girl did not marry Lord Haroun ben Hasan," the third-oldest genie objected.

"She *did* wish to be with him forever, though," said the fourth-oldest. "I think that ought to count for something."

"Of course it counts!" The youngest genie smacked his open palm with a fist. "If it did not count, then Tamar would never have been able to grant the girl's fourth wish at all! We should have seen that for ourselves. Magic always knows what it is doing."

"Better than you do," Boabdil murmured. Holding his tail like a bright banner he announced, "Let us settle this so that everyone is satisfied, even if it does bring me down to fourteen wishes. I *wish* that Nur and Haroun might be married, but only if that is what they wish, too."

"Who invited all these odd people?" the king wondered, staring at the huge crowd of rich and important people filling the largest room of his palace.

"Thirteen," murmured the drowsy cat who was curled up in Princess Nur's lap.

"Who decorated my palace so gaily?" Nur's father asked every one of his servants. They could only shrug.

"Twelve," came the sleepy purr.

"Who ordered this banquet?" the king asked the cooks. They had no idea.

"Eleven," said a voice no louder than velvet.

"Who scattered all these flowers everywhere? Who dressed my daughter in that gorgeous gown? And *who*"—the king's eyebrows came together in a look of deep bewilderment—"*who* is that richly dressed young man seated next to her?"

"Ten, nine, eight . . . No, no, that last one was none of my doing." Boabdil put one paw across his eyes and twisted himself onto his back so that Nur could stroke his stomach.

"Do not worry, Prince of a Thousand Graces," said the youngest genie, gliding up beside the king. "That excellent young man is her husband."

"Her husband?" The king scratched his head. "How did that happen?"

"Not quite in the usual way," the genie replied. "But so what? It has happened, and both of them are happy. That is what is important."

"Oh, fine." The king sank down onto a golden chair, miserable. "They can both be as happy as they like until we are all destroyed. That is just what will happen when a certain nasty old king I could name finds out that now he can never marry my daughter. What a temper he has! And what an army!"

Tamar appeared at the king's right hand. "Do you mean no one has told Your Majesty?"

"Told me what?"

"That the man your daughter has married is Lord Haroun ben Hasan, richest of the rich, kindest of the kind, and"—she paused for effect—"owner of the legendary sword of Solomon!"

Khalid drifted over from the banquet table. "No army however great, no king however bad-tempered can win against him," he added between mouthfuls of sherbet. "Your kingdom is safe forever."

"Really?" The king cheered up at once. He waddled over to the newlyweds and nearly smothered Haroun in a big bear-hug. "Welcome to the family, my son!"

While Haroun struggled in his new father's embrace, Princess Nur motioned for Tamar to join her. The female genie and Khalid sat down beside the princess, whose lap was still occupied by the sleeping Boabdil.

"What do you desire, O my Master?" Tamar whispered to Nur, for fear of disturbing him.

"I have all that I could ever desire," the princess replied. "Now I wish to set you free."

"Free—?" Joy lit up Tamar's face, and Khalid's was a reflection of her happiness.

Before either one of them could speak their thanks, Boabdil began to snort and grumble. In his dreams he muttered, "—and I used one wish to bring us all to the royal palace, so that did leave eight. Oh, it *is* good to know mathematics! Then it was seven when I made all the fountains in the city run with free wine, six when I had the genies set out feasting tables in the streets for all the people, five when I ordered musicians for the palace, four when I thought the common folk should enjoy dancing and singing too, and three was when—three was when—was when—" He twitched and growled in his sleep, trying to remember.

"The other cats, dear one," Princess Nur breathed into one pointed ear.

"Ahhhhh, yes." Boabdil's tongue stretched out in a wide pink yawn and he waved his paws in the air. "I was left with two wishes after I filled every alley in this city with fresh meat for my friends and relatives." He fell into a deeper sleep and no longer spoke.

"Two wishes are still plenty for any cat to have left,"

said Khalid, daring to tickle the sleeping creature under his upturned chin.

"Yes, except he has only one left now," said Nur. "He used the other to wish that all the dogs who think it is fun to chase cats are now ten miles outside the city walls."

"That is as good as saying he has none left," said the youngest genie. He and the other members of the council had come to gather around the sleeping cat. "He promised to use his last wish to give my friend here back his voice."

The oldest Council member nodded his head vigorously.

"He did give his word," said the second-oldest genie.

"But . . . is his promise to be trusted?" asked the third-oldest.

"Of course it is! It has to be." The fourth sounded decidedly stubborn about it. Then a small shadow of doubt crept into his mind. "After all, the beast has everything he needs— a home, food, humans to care for him. What more could an ordinary cat desire?"

Khalid decided not to remind a Council member that there was no such thing as an ordinary cat.

In Princess Nur's lap, Boabdil was talking in his sleep again. "I wonder . . . I wonder . . . I wonder what it would be like if cats were kings, if cats had wings, if people had to slink about in alleys and beg *us* to feed *them*, if dogs were small as mice, if mice came in different flavors, if cats could live among the stars, if the great Moon Cat could come down and visit me, if all the universe were ruled by cats, if—if— if—" He shifted onto his side and then spoke up as clearly as though he were fully awake: "I wish . . . I wish . . . I really, truly *wish*—!"

The princess gasped, the banquet hall fell silent, the genies froze, all magic held its breath, but the only thing that anyone heard was the unmistakable sound of one cat laughing.